AF372198

# Let's Connect!

*Thank you for taking time to read this story! I pray you enjoy it and that you will continue to follow my work as a self-published author who desires to change the world through writing! Please leave a review on Amazon at the link below, they mean everything and is always appreciated!*

God Bless,
Author Aundrya Schnel

*www.amazon.com/author/aundryaschnel*
*www.amazon.com/author/aundryarichardson*

Podcast - Ready Writers Ignite
Podcast - Mind Without Walls
Podcast - Aundrya Speaks

# Who Wants To Write A Book?

*I offer a master class where I teach men and women around the world of all ages how to write their first or next book along with the path to take for having their book published! If you have a desire to write a book, this class is for YOU! For more information and to register for the next class, please visit the website below! Thank you in advance for your support and I look forward to working with you in the near future!*

God Bless,
Aundrya


writeyourwayacademy.square.site
writeyourway@outlook.com

# TRIBUTE

*My Late Mother*

*Minister Linda Darlene Collins-Richardson*
*July 4, 1959 – June 19, 2005*


*My Late Grandmother*

*Mother Harriett Richardson*
*October 10, 1931 – February 4, 2017*

# INTRODUCTION

"I was a little surprised when you reached out to me.
I haven't seen you since high school..."
"Yeah, I know..."
"So what's up? Why do you need to talk to me after all
this time?"
"Did you really think I wasn't going to find out about
you and my wife sleeping together?"
"What? I didn't sleep with your wife!"
"You did before we got married! You hooked up with
her in high school while we were dating."
"Are you serious right now? That was a really long
time ago and it was while you were on a break."
"We were never on a break!"
"That's not what she said...."
"Whatever..."
"Look, it doesn't matter! We were kids and I know for
a fact I wasn't the only one who hooked up with your
wife in school!"
"What? Stop lying!"
"I'm not lying to you! Dee-Dee was pretty wild for a
preacher's daughter, but it's typical!"
"I'm not going to let you speak about my wife that
way!"
"Dude, I'm just saying. But again, we were kids back
then. We had a wild side, you know that! I don't
understand why you're bringing this up now!"
"Let me ask you something, did Dee ever tell you she
was pregnant in high school?"
"Oh, so that's why you're confronting me?"
"Yes! I want to know if she ever told you she was
pregnant?"

"I can't believe I'm answering this but yeah, she was.
It was our senior year of high school."
"What happened?"
"It was after we hooked up. She came to me in a panic
saying she was pregnant and that was when she said
she knew it wasn't yours because she was making you
wait until marriage..."
"Yeah, she said she was a virgin..."
"Okay, I'll pretend like you didn't say that. Listen, she
was panicked and I don't believe in abortion so I told
her that I wanted a paternity test and if the kid was
mine, I'd be there."
"What did she say when you told her that?"
"She flipped out on me! She started talking about her
parents and her sisters and how much trouble she
would be in with the church or whatever if everyone
found out she was pregnant. I asked her what she
planned to do and all she told me to do was forget
what she said because she was going to handle it."
"That was it?"
"Yes, that was it! She never brought it up again and
you weren't in my face like you are right now so I just
assumed she went and had an abortion. She was
eighteen so it's not like she would have had to tell her
parents or anything."
"I can't believe this!"
"I'm sorry man, for real. But like I said, it was a long
time ago. So wait, if Dee never told you, how did you
find out?"
"I overheard her talking about it to one of her friends.
See, I was wondering why the doctor said she was
barren and couldn't have children. I wanted details

but Dee set it to where the doctor could only give the details to her and not me. So I asked Dee and she kept acting like it was too painful for her to talk about so I left it alone. But then I heard her on the phone saying how she regretted having an abortion in high school after she hooked up with you, because now she can't have kids!"

"Dang man, that's messed up. I didn't know it went down like that. I'm sorry..."

"That's all you have to say? Do you know what this means? My wife and I haven't been married that long and I'm pastoring now so I can't leave her!"

"Oh wow, you're a pastor?"

"Yeah, I'm a pastor and I won't be able to have children of my own because my wife decided to pretend to be a virgin while being a whore with you!"

"Listen man, I know you're mad, but you need to fall back with all that! It's not my fault you weren't handling your business!"

"Don't let my title as the pastor fool you, I'm from the same hood you're from and my family has always been known to be trigger happy."

"Are you threatening me?"

"It's a promise! You ruined my life and I'm here to make you pay!"

"What about your wife? I didn't make her sleep with me!"

"Oh don't worry about Dee, I've handled that too and one day, when she finds out how I got her back for lying to me, I'll be so happy. Revenge is still sweet!"

"I thought you Christians were supposed to show
love or whatever! WOAH! DUDE, PUT THE GUN
DOWN!"
"Are you scared? I told you I wasn't playing...."
"Bro, it's not worth it! I'm sorry, I'm sorry!"
"No you're not! If you were really sorry, you would
have come clean back then instead of smiling in my
face while you screwed my woman!"
"I got it, I got it! I'm sorry, I really am! But please man,
don't kill me. I got a wife too and I have kids!"
"You have to pay for what you did!"

# THE OTHER WOMB

# PRESENT DAY

Donovan Hall grew up in Memphis, Tennessee with his mother, Leigh and he's the youngest of seven siblings; Samantha, Brandon, Cam, Wesley, Sebastian and Nichole. He's now a 37-year-old pastor in Atlanta, Georgia and he's married to his high school sweetheart, Dominique who he met when he was in fourth grade. Dominique's parents, Apostle Shawn & Lisa Ellis are pastors near the area they grew up in Memphis. Donovan's mother wasn't saved and he never knew his father, so it wasn't until Donovan met Dominique's parents for the first time in elementary school that he was introduced to God and church. Donovan built an instant bond with Shawn the first time they met and without thinking twice about it and with his mom's permission, Shawn took Donovan under his wing and began to mentor him once he knew that Donovan didn't have his father in his life. A few months into their relationship, Shawn asked Leigh if she could bring Donovan to church with him and had even offered to bring Donovan's older siblings with him too.

Leigh agreed to it as long as she never had to come to church and Shawn assured her that there was no pressure for her to attend if she allowed Donovan to go. None of Donovan's sisters and brothers were interested in attending church so Donovan always went on his own with Dominique, her parents and Dominique's two older sisters. Donovan soon began to hang on to Shawn's every word and he was excited anytime he got the opportunity to spend time with him. In addition to the leisure activities they would do together, Shawn would spend time reading the Bible to Donovan and teaching him about different stories in the Bible in addition to what he would learn in Sunday School and during the summer at vacation Bible school. Shawn believed Donovan had a call of God in his life and he felt it was his responsibility to teach him the things about God that his mother wasn't going to teach him so that he would one day answer that call. One day, all of Shawn's work and efforts with Donovan paid off when Donovan turned thirteen and gave his life to the Lord. As excited as Shawn was to see his mentee become a believer of Jesus Christ, he was concerned about what his mother's reaction would be once she found out because he knew how she felt about God and church.

Shawn worried that she would stop allowing him to take Donovan to church if she knew that he had been converted. But to his surprise, Leigh didn't have that reaction at all. She was shocked to see that her youngest child was the first one among their family to give their life to God, but she accepted Donovan's decision and told Donovan that she would allow him to continue attending church and being around Shawn as long as he didn't try telling her any scriptures he was learning from church. Donovan agreed to his mom's terms, even though it became difficult for him not to share as he continued to grow in his walk with God. As Donovan built his relationship and prayer life with God, he prayed for his mother, his siblings, his nieces and nephews every day. He really wanted them to find the same peace of God he had so they would turn from their reckless lifestyle of violence, drinking, partying and occasional drug use. Donovan and Dominique started dating when they were freshman in high school and they both agreed to follow her parents' rule by not having sex until they were married. By that time, Dominique had been saved for about as long as he had so he didn't think he would have anything to worry about, even if temptation came. But Donovan later found out that Dominique wasn't as committed as he thought after they were married and learned that Dominique was barren and was not able to have children. By this time, Donovan and Dominique had relocated to Atlanta and became the senior pastors at the church that Dominique's father was the overseer for. He was devastated that he wouldn't be able to have children of his own, because had desired for a long time to one day become a father.

Donovan loved Dominique very much and he didn't intend on holding it against her and agreed to remain faithful in his marriage. That was until one day when he came home early and Dominique didn't hear him walk inside because she was in her office talking to her best friend. Donovan walked down the hall towards the office and as he approached the door, he heard Dominique say his name and mentioned a secret she had been keeping from him. Donovan was shocked to hear her say that because they usually told each other everything, so he stood outside the door and listened to her conversation as she and her best friend talked about what happened in high school while he and Dominique were dating. Dominique admitted to have sex with other guys behind his back and went on to explain that when she found out she was pregnant their senior year of high school, the only person she had been with at that time was one of the guys from the football team named Antoine Washington. Donovan was in more shock when Dominique admitted to having an abortion so that she wouldn't have to tell her parents and family that she had not only had premarital sex, but she had sex with another guy other than Donovan and was pregnant by him. With her father's status among other prominent leaders and influence in the community, a situation like that could ruin their family in more ways than one. So Dominique did what she felt was best to protect everyone's reputation, including hers. But she never considered the man she loved and it broke Donovan's heart as he heard her talk about it because he realized by some of the things she said that the abortion she had back then was the true reason behind why they weren't able to have children of their own.

 With Dominique being a doctor herself, Donovan knew she had ways to keep something like this a secret from him and had it not been for the fact that he eavesdropped on her conversation, he would have never known anything. Donovan was too upset to confront Dominique right away one weekend when he and Dominique drove home to Memphis to visit their family, Donovan went to talk to his mother alone while Dominique spent time with her parents and her sisters. He broke down in tears as he began to tell his mother what he overheard his wife say to her best friend. Donovan was counting on his mom to guide him and tell him what he should do and Leigh's advice blew Donovan away because she suggested he do the unthinkable. Leigh told him to wait a while before confronting Dominique about what he knew and get revenge on her instead. Donovan didn't understand at first why his mom suggested he get back at his wife instead of just calling her to the carpet for what she did behind his back. That was when Leigh went on to explain how this could potentially turn out bad for him if he confronted Dominique because of the fact he was pastoring a church that was owned by her parents. His salary was being paid to him by her father and Leigh explained that if Dominique got upset and went to her father first, they would find a way to turn the entire situation around on him and have him look like the bad guy when she was in the wrong.

Donovan knew what his mom was telling him but he just couldn't understand how someone who never went to church for as long as he could remember could have so much to say about the way things worked. Donovan wanted to believe his mom but he knew how close he was to Shawn and Shawn had never done anything to Donovan to make him think he couldn't trust him. As Donovan and Leigh continued talking, she dropped a bombshell when she told him that she and her siblings grew up going to church with her parents. But one day, her father found out about something illegal that the pastor was doing with the church's money and when he threatened to speak up and do something about it, the pastor found a way to not only make it look like he was laundering the money, but he had convinced her mom that he had cheated on her with a former member who left the church. The entire situation broke up their family because her mom believed the word of the pastor over her own husband and she divorced him. It wasn't until two years after the divorce and after her father had moved to a different state and remarried that she found out the truth, but by then it was too late to go back. After hearing that, Donovan understood even better why his mother suggested he get back at her instead of confronting her. With his mom's help, Donovan found a way to get back at his wife in a way that would still allow him time before confronting his wife about what he knew.

It came down to when that moment would be for Donovan to confront Dominique with what he found out. It's now been nearly fourteen years since all of this initially took place and Donovan has kept this secret between himself and his mother all these years. Donovan's half-brothers, Wesley and Sebastian and his half-sister, Nichole also live in Atlanta. Nichole and her husband, Ryan are two of the prophets at his church. Donovan's oldest nephew, Donovan "*Malik*" Hall is the head musician at his church and his oldest niece, Ashleigh is one of the praise and worship leaders at his church. Samantha is Malik and Ashleigh's mother and it was her idea to name her first son after Donovan and her first daughter after Leigh who's real name is Ashleigh. When Leigh would talk about her parents (*Donovan's grandparents*), she always mentioned how they called her Leigh for short and she decided to go by that name after they died. Malik and Ashleigh are both in their early twenties and to this day, Donovan and his family have not been able to figure out where they got their music ability from because no one in their family that he knew of had any kind of musical talent. Malik has a dual degree in Music and Business from Georgia State University and Ashleigh decided to major in Accounting and minor in Music. Malik not only sings, but he writes music and plays several instruments including the piano, organ, keyboard, drums, bass guitar and the saxophone. Ashleigh sings, writes music and she plays the keyboard too and their talent continues to blow them away because they learned on their own.

Donovan chose to keep his problems with Dominique from Nichole so she wouldn't worry, but Donovan couldn't help but wonder if she would eventually figure out what was really going on based on the questions she would ask him at times. Donovan and Nichole have always been close so she can tell when something is wrong with him, even if he tries to hide it. While Donovan continues to tell her that everything is okay, he also remembers why he ordained Nichole as a Prophet because she's always had an ability to see and discern things, even before she got saved. But Donovan felt it was best she was kept out of the loop about this because he didn't think she would understand his frustration or his reason for wanting to get back at his wife. Little did Donovan know that what he's actively working to hide would reveal and expose itself in a way he and his mom would have never anticipated.

Six months ago, Donovan thought he was ready to confront his wife with what he knew and reveal to her what he did to get back at her for lying to him all these years. But Donovan soon changed his mind one day while he was home cleaning when Dominique was out shopping and he found a copy of the life insurance policy for Dominique's father, Shawn. Donovan had never really discussed the details of his life insurance policy with him or his wife and he was curious to see what was outlined in it and decided to read it. Halfway through the documents, Donovan nearly dropped the papers when he read a particular clause in the paperwork. Donovan didn't know that Shawn had him listed as a beneficiary in the police and in his will, it stated that Donovan was going to receive a million dollars once he passed. Donovan was in total shock and more curious on why this was never told to him and it made him wonder if he was ever supposed to know. So he made the decision not to confront Shawn or Dominique about it and kept it to himself.

Since that day, Donovan can't help but wonder how this would potentially help him in the near future because Shawn was getting older and he had his share of health problems which was part of why he expanded his network of pastors that are under his ministry by ordaining two more leaders to pastor churches at two other locations. Usually when Donovan talks to Shawn, he always says that he's doing okay. But seeing him secretly listed as a beneficiary makes him wonder if things are worse than what he's chosen to share with any of them.

It was a typical Saturday afternoon with Donovan and Dominique spending time with their four godchildren; Judah, Joshua, Joseph and Justice who live in Atlanta with their mother, Dr. Nia Westbrook who was friends with him and Dominique in college. Judah just turned thirteen a month ago and he gave his life to the Lord two weeks later which had Donovan in tears because he didn't realize it would happen the same way it did with him when he was that age. Judah has always been mature for his age and it was part of why Donovan made him one of the praise and worship leaders at their church where he leads other singers much older than him. Joshua, Joseph and Justice are younger than Judah but know how to sing as well. Nia knows how to sing so she teaches and rehearses with them at home. Joshua and Joseph have been learning how to play different instruments from Malik so Donovan knows it will only be a matter of time before they're able to play for services just like Malik and the other musicians in their ministry.

Justice's interests on the other hand are a little different from her brothers. She enjoys singing but Donovan noticed that when she's at church with them, she loves to sit close with the intercessors at their ministry. He didn't give it much thought at first until one Sunday when Nichole preached and she said that Justice would carry a passion for intercession at a young age and that God would use her to break chains off a generation as well as her family. After Donovan and Dominique dropped their godchildren back home with Nia, Donovan was going to drop his wife off at home before heading over to see Malik at his apartment. But Dominique insisted he come inside so they could talk and continue making preparations for the annual summer conference that was coming up in three months.

"This conference is making my head hurt. Did we really have to host the conference this year?" Donovan asked as he and Dominique sat outside on the patio.

"Baby, I don't know why you're still asking that at this point. You know my dad wanted to do it in Atlanta this year for networking reasons. The people he knows with money are here so we're having it here this year." Dominique said.

"I know. I guess I just thought we wouldn't be under so much stress since our staff is in charge of getting everything ready for the conference." Donovan replied.

"Yeah speaking of that, is this email you sent me the report update from the last staff meeting you had?" Dominique asked as she looked at her laptop.

"Yeah, we met on Thursday. Why?" Donovan asked.

"No reason, I was just making sure this was the most recent report. Everything seems to be going according to plan. I'm looking forward to the women's breakfast we're doing this year for the conference!" Dominique, smiling a little.

"Oh yeah, that's one of the morning sessions right?" Donovan asked.

"Yeah, according to this it's on Friday morning. Your sister is the speaker so I know it will be awesome!" Dominique said as Donovan nodded.

"That's right, she's the only one of our in-house leaders speaking for the conference. Everyone else is from out of town." Donovan told her.

"Yeah, I had to make sure the other leaders were okay about that and didn't take it personally. They said they were fine and I explained that the speaker we were going to get double booked so we asked Nichole if she would speak to avoid canceling it all together." Dominique said.

"I understand." Donovan replied.

"Babe, can I ask you something?" Dominique asked.

"Of course..."

"Is it me or does it seem like Nia has become distant with us over the years?" Dominique asked as Donovan paused and thought for a moment.

"Well, I can't say yes or no to that, baby. I mean, I only really talk to Nia when we're going to pick up the kids. She doesn't go out with you and Cindy anymore?" Donovan asked.

"Not much. It's like she hangs out with us just enough for us not to ask her about it, but we've known Nia long enough to know when she's being distant. Thing is, Cindy and I can't figure out what her problem is." Dominique said.

"Well, she's your friend. I think you and Cindy should go out with her one day and just ask her. I mean you never know, she could be dealing with something and just doesn't know how to talk about it." Donovan said as Dominique nodded.

"That's true. I mean most of her family is here minus her sister who's in Florida so it's not like she's alone. Yeah, we will talk to her. Let's get back to this. Who is Uncle Reece?" Dominique asked as Donovan started laughing.

"You really don't know who Uncle Reece is?" Donovan asked.

"I asked, didn't I? Why are you laughing at me?" she asked, laughing a little.

"Your reaction was funny. Uncle Reece is a gospel rap artist. He and a few others will be here for the youth concert and service on Friday night." Donovan replied.

"So they're going to be over at the other sanctuary I'm assuming." Dominique said.

"Yes, of course." Donovan said.

"So is that why we have an entire team of musicians other than ours for that night?" Dominique asked.

"Yes, that's right. You know our musicians are young minus Malik and Ashleigh, and they're all going to want to be at the concert and at the service too. Malik will be on the keys Friday night, Judah is playing the drums, Ashleigh's leading praise and worship and I think Trey and his guys will be backing them up too. But it's just for Friday though." Donovan told her.

"Okay, well this all looks pretty good from what I can see. I think our biggest stress will be keeping the other network pastors and their wives entertained when they come the weekend before." Dominique said.

"Yeah, that's true. We can just figure that out when they get here though, it doesn't have to be anything too special." Donovan said.

"Okay, that's fine." she said.

"Alright, are we done?" Donovan asked.

"Yeah, why? You still need to leave?" Dominique asked.

"Yes, I do..."

"The musicians have probably gone home by now, baby." Dominique said.

"Yes, they are. Malik texted me a few moments ago so I'm going to shower and change my clothes and head to my brother's birthday party. Sebastian turns forty today and Wesley planned something for him at his house and I promised I would come." Donovan said.

"Of course, have fun. Tell him I said happy birthday." Dominique said as Donovan stood to his feet.

"Sure, I will." Donovan replied.

"So Wesley didn't ask you to help plan your own brother's fortieth birthday party?" Dominique asked, surprised as Donovan laughed a little.

"Wesley said he would just invite me to come because he didn't think I could plan a good party since I'm a pastor." Donovan said as Dominique started laughing.

"Your brothers are too much! So will there be women at this party?" Dominique asked.

"Oh my God, I knew you were going to ask me that. Babe, I'm not sure and if there are, they will be there for my brothers and all of their friends, not me." Donovan said.

"You say that like you're not attractive or something, Donovan." Dominique said as Donovan laughed again.

"Baby, I'm just saying you don't have anything to worry about." Donovan said as Dominique paused for a moment before responding.

"Please don't get in any pictures or videos with whatever women are at the party. All it takes is the wrong photo or video to ruin the church's and my parents' reputation." Dominique said.

"Dominique, don't you think I know this? I hang out with my brothers all the time. I know!" Donovan said, sternly as Dominique sighed and nodded.

"I'm sorry, I'm not trying to hassle you. But you tell me all the time how wild Wesley and Sebastian are. I just don't want them getting you caught up in anything crazy." Dominique replied.

"I understand, but they won't. I promise. They know I can only go so far with them so don't worry." Donovan said as he kissed Dominique on her forehead before walking back inside the house.

"I love you, Donovan." Dominique said as he walked to the patio door and turned to look at her.

"I love you too." Donovan replied.

Donovan quickly showered and changed his clothes before getting ready to drive to his brother, Wesley's house for his brother Sebastian's fortieth birthday party. Based on how Wesley had been describing his plans for the party, he couldn't tell if this was supposed to be a surprise party for Sebastian or not, so he didn't say anything about the party to him just in case. Even though Donovan always managed to assure his wife that he wasn't talking to other women when he was out with his brothers, it wasn't the truth. Wesley and Sebastian sell houses and work in finance so they both have big houses and are known for having the wildest parties. Donovan hooked up with some of these women at the parties from time to time without his wife ever finding out about it. Donovan was living this double life not realizing the level of impact his lifestyle was having on Wesley and Sebastian who aren't saved. Donovan wasn't telling the truth when he told Dominique she didn't help Wesley plan Sebastian's party, he had a major hand in it. Wesley and Donovan split the cost to hire six exotic dancers to perform at the party.

Donovan arrived at Wesley's house just as the party was starting and just before the dancers they hired arrived. He was standing near the kitchen next to Wesley having a drink when the girls walked in. After they were inside, Donovan told Wesley to pull the dancer wearing the black attire aside and bring her to a room in the back because he needed to talk to her. Wesley didn't know what was going on but he figured Donovan would tell him once they were in the back so he did as he asked. Sebastian was on the dance floor drinking and dancing with two women while everyone else at the party continued dancing and listening to the music.

"Alright bro, I got her back here like you asked. What the hell's going on?" Wesley asked confused as Donovan walked over and locked the door.
"Did you boys want a private dance?" the dancer asked as she started smiling.
"Yes!" Wesley said, excitedly as Donovan stopped him.
"No, not right now. She can dance with her friends in a minute if she does what I say." Donovan said sternly as the young woman's expression changed.
"What are you talking about?" she asked.
"You're Camilla Lawrence, right?" Donovan asked.

"You know her whole name?" Wesley asked, confused.
"Yeah, how did you know my name?" she asked, concerned.
"Your ex-boyfriend, Malik is our nephew and he told me that you're still stalking him and trying to make him take care of your daughter knowing damn well the test proved it wasn't his!" Donovan said as Wesley pulled out his gun and held at his side.

"Oh is that right? You're trying to trap Malik?" Wesley asked as Camilla became nervous when she saw Wesley's gun.

"Guys, it's not what you think. I just wanted to work things out with Malik." Camilla said.

"Don't play games with me, Camilla. I didn't know this until after the fact but you showed up at my church last week and sat in the back with your little girl to distract Malik. Have you lost your mind?" Donovan asked.

"Wow, I thought you looked familiar. So you're the pastor and you're here with dancers?" Camilla asked with a smirk.

"I'm the one asking the questions here, Camilla. You're dancing for my brother's birthday party so I'm here to support him and if you even think about trying to put me on blast, your daughter won't have a mother." Donovan said, sternly.

"Are you threatening me?" she asked.

"No, it's a promise if you say anything or if you ever show up at my church again. Stay away from my church and my nephew, you got it? I won't warn you again. If my nephew tells me you're still bothering him, you're going to deal with his uncles." Donovan said.

"Lady, don't let my brother's title as a pastor fool you. Our family is a dangerous one and if Malik's mom knew what you were doing, they would be here right now ready to hurt you without thinking twice." Wesley said.

"Yeah, we're being nice enough to warn you but I don't know Wesley, I think we might need to show this one we mean business. What do you think?" Donovan asked.

"Yeah, let's show her but not too much. She still gotta do what we paid her to do." Wesley replied as Donovan nodded and punched Camilla in her stomach causing her to fall to the floor and frantically try to catch her breath as Wesley and Donovan stood over her.

"Okay! Okay! I'll leave Malik alone and I promise I won't talk and you won't see me again after tonight unless you request a dancer." Camilla said as she laid on the floor in tears holding her stomach.

"Yeah, I thought you might change your tune after that gut punch. If you weren't dancing tonight, I would give you more, but don't think it can't be arranged. I have your name, your address and I know what club you're at. If you care about your daughter you will do what we tell you and not mess with Malik ever again!" Donovan said as Camilla slowly got up from the floor.

"Okay, fine..."

"Alright, fix yourself up so we can go back to the party." Donovan said as Wesley grabbed Camilla and rushed her into the hallway as Donovan locked the door behind them and headed back to the party.

"Bro, you should have told me about this chick. I would have picked a different dancer." Wesley said as he and Donovan came downstairs.

"I wanted her to come so we could let her know what time it was. She's coming out now so I think we're ready to start the show." Donovan said as Wesley nodded and walked over to the microphone on the stage set up in the living room where everyone was dancing.

"I was wondering where you two went! This part is too wild and there's dancers too?" Sebastian asked as he took another drink of wine.

"Yeah man, you only turn forty once! We had to do it right." Wesley replied as he and Sebastian slapped hands.

"I appreciate you guys man, thanks! It's too bad Cam and Brandon couldn't be here. Cam constantly has to watch Brandon, he hasn't been the same since his boys died." Sebastian told them as they nodded.

"Yeah, it's pretty bad. If it wasn't for that incident that happened the week Cam was here, we would have told him to let Mom and Samantha watch him." Donovan replied as Wesley and Sebastian nodded.

"So Donovan, your wife let you out the house tonight?" Sebastian asked as Wesley started laughing.

"My wife doesn't run anything, trust me." Donovan said.

"Man, you know you got a curfew!" Sebastian replied as Donovan started laughing.

"Not at all! I know how to keep my wife in the dark about stuff, can't say the same for her though."

Donovan said as Wesley and Sebastian glanced at each other.

"What do you mean by that?" Wesley asked as Donovan shook his head.

"I'll tell you later." Donovan said.

"How about you tell us sometime next week." Sebastian said.

"What's next week?" Donovan asked.

"Nothing special, I just think it's time we had a conversation." Sebastian replied as Donovan looked confused.

"What do we need to talk about? Is something wrong?" Donovan asked.

"That's what we want you to tell us bro. We know something is up with you." Wesley said.

"You two sound just like Nichole, she said the same thing. I'm fine." Donovan replied.

"No you're not. Listen, you can hide from Nichole but not your big brothers." Wesley said as Donovan sighed and paused for a moment before responding.

"I'm not going to go into details right now, but something has been going on. I've kept it to myself all this time but I knew I would talk to you guys about it at some point. I've just been waiting for the right time." Donovan said.

"See, we knew it! We knew something was going on." Sebastian replied.

"Guys, we can hang out next week but I don't know if I'm ready to talk about it." Donovan said.

"Alright man, no pressure. But you're going to tell us though, right?" Wesley asked.

"Yes, I will at the right moment since I'm going to need your help." Donovan said as Wesley and Sebastian glanced at each other.

"You're going to need our help? Is someone coming after you or something?" Wesley asked.

"It's complicated, but I'll talk to you about it at the right time, I promise." Donovan said as Sebastian and Wesley nodded.

"Okay Donovan, you know we got your back for whatever so just let us know." Wesley said as the three of them slapped hands and hugged each other.

"I appreciate it guys, thank you." Donovan replied.

"Alright, cool! Where did you two go earlier with that dancer? Did she give you some head or something?" Sebastian asked as Donovan explained why they were in the back. "Oh wow, she's been stalking Malik?"

"Yeah she was, she couldn't move on once that paternity test proved her little girl wasn't his. But we roughed her up a bit so I don't think we're going to have any more problems." Donovan said.

"Bro, I like this side of you. You're a whole pastor but you got your tough streak just like your family! I knew you didn't change all the way." Sebastian said as Donovan laughed a little.

"Yeah, I'm still from the hood and I still believe in handling your business when someone crosses you up." Donovan said.

"I heard that! So is that what you're waiting to talk to us about? Someone crossed you?" Wesley asked.

"Yeah, it's something like that but I found a way to get them back. But it's complicated and I'll tell you the whole story at a later time." Donovan said.

"So you've kept whatever this is to yourself all this time?" Sebastian asked.

"Well, Mom is the only other person who knows. What I did was after she gave me advice." Donovan said.

"Oh wow, you let Mom advise you? Bro, I love our mom but you know how crazy she is! She's ruthless!" Wesley said.

"I know, but the situation was messed up and I needed someone to talk to me who would tell me how to make the revenge sweet and she helped me do it. Some of it, anyway." Donovan replied.

"Who are you trying to get revenge on?" Wesley asked.

"I'll tell you that later too, but it will shock you." Donovan said as his brothers nodded and continued drinking and watching the dancers perform on stage.

The next morning when Donovan arrived at church, he went to his office to look at something on his computer before service started and people started to arrive. Donovan was still pretty tired from Sebastian's party last night, but he was relieved because his assistant pastor was speaking today and he wasn't going to have to worry about preaching.

Moments later, Donovan's nephew, Malik came into his office after Donovan texted him asking Malik to come talk to him when he arrived at church.

"Hey Uncle Donovan, you wanted to see me?" Malik asked as he stood at the door.

"Yeah Malik, have a seat." Donovan said as Malik shut the door behind him and sat at his desk.

"What's going on?" Malik asked.

"I'll start by saying that I handled that little situation you told me about with Camilla." Donovan said.

"You did? You saw Camilla? Where?" Malik asked, shocked.

"You're asking too many questions, just know I saw her and you shouldn't have to worry about her ever coming around you again." Donovan said as Malik nodded and sighed in relief.

"Thank you Uncle Donovan, I appreciate it." Malik said.

"You're welcome Malik but listen, I need you to be more careful from now on with these girls you decide to hook up with. Now you know me, I'm not going to get all in your business and I don't care what you do when you're not here. But you can't have your outside drama showing up at my church and as much as I love you, I will not chase down every chick who decides they want to stalk you." Donovan replied as Malik nodded in agreement.

"Yes sir, I understand. I had no idea Camilla was going to be crazy enough to show up at the church like that so I was just as shocked as you were.

But you're right, I do have to be more careful from now on and I will." Malik replied as Donovan nodded.

"Okay, good. So who's leading worship today?" Donovan asked, changing the subject.

"I think it's Judah's turn to lead today. I just saw him, Joshua, Joseph and Justice walk in with Aunt Dominique when I was coming inside." Malik said.

"Okay, that's fine. Are you and Ashleigh still going to Miami to see your sisters?" Donovan asked.

"Yes sir, we're leaving tomorrow and we should be back by Friday. We can't wait to see them, it's been a while." Malik said.

"That's true, it has been a minute. I still don't understand why they chose to go all the way to Miami alone after they turned eighteen." Donovan said as Malik paused for a moment before responding.

"Ashleigh and I finally know the truth behind that move. I'll tell you as long as you promise not to tell anyone, especially my mom or Grandma." Malik said.

"I won't tell them anything, what is it?" Donovan asked.

"Tiffany and Tracey found their biological father and he lives in Miami with his wife." Malik said as Donovan reacted to what Malik told him.

"Are you serious? They found their dad? How? Are they sure it's him?" Donovan asked.

"Yeah, they said they're sure. When they found him, they had a DNA test done and it came back saying he was their father. We asked them how they knew where to look and Tracey said that she and Tiffany ended up overhearing some conversation our mom was having with Grandma one day about their dad and she said his name. They wrote it down and ended up finding him on social media. Isn't that crazy?" Malik asked.

"Yeah, that's really crazy. So let me guess, Tiffany and Tracey resent your mom for not telling them the truth about their father and that's why it takes an act of congress to get them to go home to visit. Is that right?" Donovan asked as Malik nodded.

"Yeah, that's exactly why. They of course still see Ashleigh and me, and I know they've come to Memphis before to check on Uncle Brandon but they've pretty cut our mom off. Ashleigh and I are trying to talk them into talking to our mom and telling them the truth so they can really express how they feel." Malik said.

"Well hopefully they will come around with that." Donovan replied as he started typing on his computer.

"Uncle Donovan, if you have another minute, I need to tell you something else." Malik said as Donovan stopped typing and glanced at him.

"Your entire tone changed when you said that just now, Malik. Of course I have another minute for you, what's wrong?" Donovan asked as he walked around and sat in a chair across from him.

"I'm not trying to start anything, especially with the summer conference coming up but Ashleigh just texted me a minute ago and said she had something come up and won't be at church today. So I think I should tell you what's been going on." Malik said as Donovan glanced at his phone to see if Ashleigh reached out to him too.

"Okay, she texted you but didn't reach out to me about missing church? I'm confused. So what do you need to tell me? Do you know where Ashleigh is?" Donovan asked.

"Yes sir, I know where she is. More than likely she's leading worship today at Pastor Singleton's church in Decatur." Malik said as Donovan's expression changed.

"Pastor Singleton as in Cedric Singleton, III? She's at his church?" Donovan asked as Malik nodded.

"Yes sir, I think that's where she is." Malik replied.

"Okay, so what makes you think she's there of all places?" Donovan asked as Malik sighed and paused for a moment before responding.

"Pastor Singleton has been emailing Ashleigh and me about coming to be over the music department at his church. He's been offering us all this money to leave you and come to him." Malik said as Donovan looked surprised.

"Are you serious right now? Malik, how long has this been going on and why didn't you tell me before today? He shouldn't be contacting either of you!" Donovan said, sternly.

"I'm sorry for not telling you before now, Uncle Donovan. Ashleigh and I had been turning down all of his offers and we told him we weren't leaving your ministry. So since neither of us were planning to support him, we didn't want to bother you about it since we know how you feel about him." Malik said.

"I get that but from now on, you come to me no matter what. Okay?" Donovan asked.

"Yes sir..."

"I guess I shouldn't be too surprised that Cedric is trying this. I know he's still bitter because my father-in-law chose me to lead the Atlanta location instead of him." Donovan said as Malik reacted to what Donovan told him.

"Oh wow, is that what happened?" Malik asked.

"Yes..."

"Do you know why he turned him down?" Malik asked.

"I don't know all the details, I just know he said Cedric couldn't be trusted. Now I thought you just said that you and Ashleigh turned Cedric down. Why would you suspect Ashleigh is over there now?" Donovan asked as Malik pulled out his phone and handed it to Donovan to show him an email.

"Pastor Singleton sent that to Ashleigh and I on Friday. I didn't respond and Ashleigh said she didn't say anything either because we told him no a million times. But that's the most money he's ever offered us and all of a sudden today, Ashleigh's not here. I think she's there doing what he asked for so she can get paid." Malik said as Donovan shook his head in disbelief.

"This is ridiculous! Ten grand a piece to do praise and worship at his church? That's three times the amount I'm paying you and Cedric knows that, that's why he offered you so much." Donovan said as Malik nodded.

"Well, it looks like Ashleigh decided to bite the bait." Malik told him.

"Can I ask you something?" Donovan asked.

"Yes sir..."

"I know we're family but this is a lot of money. You weren't tempted to take Cedric up on his offer?" Donovan asked.

"Yes, I was tempted but I wasn't going to leave you over some money. I really don't even know Pastor Singleton like that but I trust you, Uncle Donovan and I always have. No amount of money would make me turn on you after everything you've done for over the years." Malik said as he and Donovan hugged each other.

"I appreciate that, Malik. Regardless of what people may say, loyalty really does take you far." Donovan said as Malik nodded.

"That's what my mom always told us too. I guess Ashleigh hasn't been listening. She's going to be mad at me for telling you but she knows she's not right." Malik said as Donovan nodded.

"You will be the furthest thing away from her mind once I'm done with her. I'm going to reach out to Ashleigh later on and confront her about it." Donovan replied as he sent a text message on his phone.

"Okay..."

"Alright Malik, thanks for the heads up. You can head inside, I'll be there in a moment." Donovan said.

"Since you said you were going to confront Ashleigh, there's something else I want to mention to you if that's okay." Malik said.

"There's more? Okay Malik, I'm listening. What do you want to tell me?" Donovan asked.

"It may not be anything serious but a month ago, Ashleigh and I almost got into an argument about you." Malik replied as Donovan's expression changed.

"You were arguing about me? Why? That doesn't even make any sense." Donovan told him.

"Ashleigh came to my place one day to look over some music and this story came on the news about some pastor who got arrested for something. Ashleigh then made this comment about you having secrets that you hide behind your title as the pastor." Malik said as Donovan reacted to what he told him.

"She said that about her own uncle?" Donovan asked, disgusted.

"Yes, she did! I didn't know why she was saying it and I didn't want to know. I just responded and told her to never say anything like that again because you were different and you weren't like these other preachers." Malik said as Donovan nodded.

"I may need to pay Miss Ashleigh a visit today after church. Is there anything else you want to tell me, Malik?" Donovan asked.

"No sir, that was it. I promise." Malik said.

Donovan managed to maintain his composure while he was talking to Malik, but he was nervous about the comments that Malik said Ashleigh made about him. Donovan does have his share of secrets that he does a pretty good job of hiding without them interfering with what he does as a pastor. But Ashleigh's comments were concerning to Donovan and he couldn't help but wonder what she knew or it was that was making her feel the way she did towards him. Donovan also wondered if she expressed her frustration to Pastor Singleton and worried about what could happen if she did because Pastor Singleton has been watching his church extra closely ever since he was turned down by Donovan's father-in-law to be included in his preaching network. After service was over, Donovan spent the time he normally spends talking and catching up with his members before leaving.

Donovan was in luck today because he didn't have any scheduled meetings with anyone and he was relieved when Dominique reminded him that she was going to another service in a couple of hours to support her two older sisters who were speaking at a local church in the city. Donovan took Judah, Joshua, Joseph and Judah out to eat before taking them back home to their mother. After taking them home for the evening, Donovan drove to Sandy Springs to visit Ashleigh at her apartment after Malik texted Donovan to let him know that Ashleigh was home. Donovan arrived at Ashleigh's apartment and knocked on her door. He could tell by her facial expression when she opened the door, that she was surprised to see him. But Ashleigh knew why he was coming to see her and she figured now would be as good of a time as any to tell Donovan some news that was probably going to be hard for him to hear.

"Hey Uncle Donovan, I was just about to call you." Ashleigh said as she handed Donovan some water and they sat in the living room.

"Yeah right, Ashleigh. Let's just cut to the chase, you know why I'm here right?" Donovan asked.

"You're here because I wasn't at church today and I didn't text you to tell you where I was. Right?" Ashleigh asked.

"Yeah, that's part of it. But see it's where you went that concerns me. You were at Cedric Peterson's church today?" Donovan asked as Ashleigh was caught off guard by his question.

"I'm going to kill Malik for opening his big mouth." Ashleigh said as they sat down at her dining room table.

"So he was right? That's where you were today?" Donovan asked as Ashleigh sighed and shook her head.

"Yes, Uncle Donovan, that's where I was." Ashleigh replied, shyly.

"Not that you've missed church that often but you normally tell me when you're not going to be there. But this time you told Malik and didn't say anything to me." Donovan said.

"I didn't tell you where I was going because I knew how you felt about Pastor Singleton and I wasn't about to argue with you." Ashleigh said.

"So is it true that he's been reaching out to you and Malik and making offers for you both to come do the music at his church?" Donovan asked.

"Wow, I really can't believe Malik said all of this to you. Yes, he did and on Friday he made an offer I couldn't refuse. That's why I was there today." Ashleigh said.

"Is this your way of telling me that you've left my church and gone to one of our biggest rivals?" Donovan asked, sternly.

"Uncle Donovan, I was planning to come meet with you one on one and tell you but I guess I have to do it now. I signed an agreement with Pastor Singleton that confirms what he offered to Malik and me on Friday in the email." Ashleigh said as Donovan looked disappointed.

"Wow Ashleigh, really? So loyalty and family means nothing to you? Malik turned down the offer, why can't you?" Donovan asked, sternly.

"You and I both know that Malik has producers looking at him and they're throwing money at him left and right. So he can stay your musician and still get paid what he's worth. I wasn't getting that same opportunity, Uncle Donovan! Yes, Malik tried to include me with him when he went to certain meetings and events, but I wasn't what they wanted. They wanted him, not me!" Ashleigh said.

"So you think you're going to get a record deal now because you're at Cedric's church?" Donovan asked.

"No Uncle Donovan, I know I will! Things are already in the works and that was another reason I went to sing at his church today. Two producers came to visit and Pastor Singleton told them about me and they were interested in hearing me sing so he thought today would be the perfect time." Ashleigh said.

"Wow, so I guess you have it all figured out huh?" Donovan asked.

"I'm just doing what I have to do to get ahead. Isn't that what you, Mom and Grandma always taught us?" Ashleigh asked.

"Yeah but we also taught you to never turn your back on your family either, and you seemed to have forgotten that lesson!" Donovan asid.

"That's not fair Uncle Donovan and you know it. So I guess all you care about is what I do to push your vision along, you don't care what happens to me or Malik for that matter! See Malik has found a way to make you happy and himself but I refuse to work that hard!" Ashleigh replied.

"You're really bold to make a move like this knowing what I've done for you. So now my mom isn't enough for you? My money was plenty when you were in college and my money kept you from having to dance on a pole for tuition money! How soon we forget!" Donovan said, angrily.

"I'm your niece and you know my father isn't around. I thought you were helping me because you wanted to!" Ashleigh said.

"I did, Ashleigh! But maybe I should have let you make it happen at the strip club instead of offering my help." Donovan said as Ashleigh paused for a moment before responding.

"You don't mean that!" she said.

"Yeah, I do! I meant every word and if the check Cedric gives you clears, I want my money." Donovan said as Ashleigh looked surprised.

"What? You want me to pay you back what you gave me for school? I don't have that right now and even if I did, there was no agreement saying I had to pay you back!" Ashleigh said.

"Well, let today's conversation be a verbal agreement. You're going to pay me back!" Donovan replied as Ashleigh laughed, sarcastically.

"I'll see what my mom says about that." Ashleigh said.

"You're 22-years-old, Ashleigh. You don't need to bring your mom into this. Besides, she would flip if she knew I had to save you from dancing on a stripper pole!" Donovan said.

"So are you saving those girls you saw last night, Uncle Donovan?" Ashleigh asked as Donovan's expression changed.

"What are you talking about?" he asked, confused.

"One of my friends from school didn't have an uncle with money to help her out this semester so she dances part-time. She was at Uncle Sebastian's surprise birthday party last night and she told me she saw you. Imagine my surprise and disgust when I realized my uncle, the pastor, was at a party with strippers!" Ashleigh said, enraged.

"I was celebrating Sebastian's birthday and that was it! I didn't dance with any of those girls, I don't care what your little whore of a friend told you!" Donovan said.

"So is my friend lying about what you and Uncle Wesley did to Camilla? Yeah Uncle Donovan, she saw the bruises that she tried covering up. Did you two rape her?" Ashleigh asked as Donovan reacted to what she said.

"Rape? No! Are you seriously asking me that right now? All we did was have a conversation with Camilla because she was stalking Malik!" Donovan replied as Ashleigh shook her head.

"I expect Uncle Sebastian and Uncle Wesley to have strippers, they're not saved. But I can't believe you stayed there knowing these girls were going to dance naked for you. Did Aunt Dominique know about the strippers?" Ashleigh asked with a smirk .

"If you even think about telling my wife anything, I'll kill you myself and nobody will find you!" Donovan said.

"Wow Uncle Donovan, why so aggressive? Afraid Uncle Dominique will find out your little secrets and realize she made a mistake marrying you when she could have had a rich doctor who makes what she makes if not more?" Ashleigh asked.

"What are you talking about? I don't have any secrets, Ashleigh." Donovan replied.

"Oh, but you do! You have many of them and that's another reason why I'm leaving your church, Uncle Donovan. You don't have integrity. I may not have all the details but there's one major secret of yours that I know would destroy your whole church and your family if it came out." Ashleigh said with a smirk as Donovan quickly walked over to Ashleigh and slammed her against the wall as she screamed.

"SHUT-UP!" he said.

"Uncle Donovan, you're hurting me! Stop!" Ashleigh replied in tears.

"I SAID SHUT-UP!"

"Uncle Donovan, please let me go!" she said.

"Oh so now you want me to let you go after what you just said to me? Don't let this suit and this title as the pastor fool you, Ashleigh! I am my mother's son and I'll come after anyone who thinks they will sabotage everything I've worked my ass off to build!" Donovan said as he abruptly released his grip from Ashleigh as she fell to the floor and began crying hysterically.

"JUST GO!" she said, enraged.

"Oh no, I'm not going anywhere yet! What's this secret?" Donovan said as he pulled his chair up to where Ashleigh was sitting on the floor.

"Just forget it!" she said.

"Girl, I'm not playing with you!" Donovan said as he pulled out his gun and held it in his hand. "You better tell me what you were about to say!"

"You have a gun?" Ashleigh asked, shocked.

"Yes, I have a gun! You still think it's a game?" Donovan asked.

"But I'm your niece!" Ashleigh said as Donovan laughed, sarcastically.

"Yeah, and I'm your uncle. But you didn't let that stop you from betraying me and going to Cedric's church. So at this point, you're my enemy and just another target if you get in my way. Now cut the crap and tell me what this secret is!" Donovan said as Ashleigh sighed in frustration and shook her head.

"Can I get up first?" she asked.

"No you can't! You're going to sit right there where you are, beneath me!" Donovan said.

"I can't believe you! You really think you're going to get away with what you did, but the truth will come out sooner or later!" Ashleigh said.

"What truth, Ashleigh?" Donovan asked.

"Do you remember a couple of weeks ago when you asked me to watch your godchildren at the last minute because you had something come up while their mom was out of town?" Ashleigh asked.

"Yeah, I remember. I left them with you and Malik." Donovan replied.

"Well, Malik got a call to go do something at the studio so they ended up with me for a few hours." Ashleigh said as Donovan looked confused.

"Okay, so what? Why are you telling me this now?" he asked.

"I don't understand why no one else was suspicious of this, especially Aunt Dominique but the older the kids get, the more I see some of your features in them. Now I know they're your godchildren, but I couldn't help but wonder if they were your real children." Ashleigh said.

"They're not!" Donovan said, defensively.

"Oh, but they are! See, I took the straw you were drinking out of before you left my apartment that day and I took the kids' toothbrushes from their bag and I asked someone for a favor. They ran a test for me and it was confirmed that Judah, Joshua, Joseph and Justice are your biological children and I have the results on my phone. You still want to lie to me?" Ashleigh asked as Donovan paused for a moment before responding.

"I really can't believe you did that, Ashleigh. That was none of your business!" Donovan said, sternly.

"You're right, it's none of my business. But I'm glad I did it because you clearly weren't going to tell the truth! How could you do this to Dominique when you know she's barren? Were you that upset about not being able to have children of your own?" Ashleigh asked, disgusted.

"There's more to the story Ashleigh, you don't know everything and you really should have stayed out of this!" Donovan replied.

"What's missing?" Ashleigh asked.

"I'm not telling you that! Now how much do I have to pay you to keep this quiet?" Donovan asked as Ashleigh started laughing sarcastically.

"I don't want your money, Uncle Donovan." Ashleigh told him.

"Well if you want to live, you will destroy those results and keep your mouth shut! Who have you told so far?" Donovan asked, sternly.

"I haven't told anyone and the friend who did the test for me doesn't even know anything about you being a pastor or any of that! Trust me, I wanted to blast you when I found out the truth but I have to think about those kids and how confused they would be if they found out that the man they've called *"Uncle Donnie"* all these years was really the man they should be calling their father. Have you even thought about that?" Ashelgih asked.

"Yes Ashleigh, I've thought about that! Don't stand here, get self-righteous with me like you don't have a past! I wonder what Cedric would say if he found out his new praise and worship leader was a stripper for a short period of time." Donovan said.

"You wouldn't!" she said.

"Try me and see! Cedric and I may not be friends but if I told him that about you, he wouldn't think twice before cutting you off. So you decide what you want to do." Donovan said as Ashleigh shook her head.

"When are you going to tell Aunt Dominique and your kids the truth? I can't believe you were sneaking around with their mom all this time! Isn't she friends with Aunt Dominique?" Ashleigh asked.

"Yeah, she is. But it's payback, you wouldn't understand." Donovan said as Ashleigh became confused.

"Payback? What do you mean by payback?" Ashleigh asked.

"Like I said Ashleigh, this isn't your business and when I leave here, you need to act like you never found any of this out. You want to sing and make all this money at Cedric's church, do it! But don't even think about exposing me or you will be as good as dead, and I could care less about you being my niece." Donovan said as Ashleigh sighed in frustration.

"Okay fine, I won't talk." Ashleigh said.

"Ashleigh, I'm serious. I really don't want to hurt you but if you try to get in my way, I will. I've done it before." Donovan replied as Ashleigh's expression changed.

"You've done it before? You've killed someone before?" Ashleigh asked, concerned.

"No, forget what I said. Just keep your mouth shut, okay? I have to go." Donovan said as he put his gun back at his side under his jacket before leaving Ashleigh's house and driving away in his truck.

Donovan drove through the streets of Atlanta with his hands gripping the wheel as he thought about the fact that his niece uncovered his darkest secret about being the biological father of his godchildren. When Donovan overheard Dominique tell one of her other friends that got pregnant their senior year of high school by a guy she slept with named Antoine Washington, he was devastated because she always led him to believe that she was a virgin who was waiting until her wedding night to have sex. But it turned out to only be a front that Dominique put on for her overprotective parents and judgemental older sisters. Donovan thought he was going to be willing to forgive Dominique for lying to him once he confronted her about it until she dropped another bombshell while talking to her friend and explained that the abortion she had in high school that year was the cause of her being barren. Dominique knew long before they got married that she would not be able to conceive children and she never told Donovan the truth, even though she knew how badly he wanted kids of his own once they were married.

It was Donovan's mother Leigh, who suggested that Donovan get revenge on Dominique instead of simply confronting her. At first Donovan didn't know how to get back at his wife in a way that would compare to the amount of pain she caused him, and that was when Leigh told him to hit her where it would hurt her the most. Donovan gave it more thought and Nia Westbrook came to mind. Donovan and Dominique met Nia the summer before they started their freshman year of college and Donovan always wondered if Nia had a secret liking to him, but he never asked her about it. Six months into their first year of college, Donovan ran into Nia at the library and she asked him for help with an assignment she was working on. It was late at night and they were on the seventh floor in a secluded area and that was when Nia kissed him as he attempted to help her with what she was working on. Nia wanted to kiss him again but Donovan stopped her and said he didn't want to cheat on Dominique. Even though Nia didn't try coming on to Donovan after that, Donovan knew she wanted to be with him. But he did his best to never give Nia a reason to think there was a chance for them being anything more than friends and always making it clear that Dominique was the woman he wanted to be with. When Donovan's mother made her suggestion to him, all of those things came back to his memory and it made him angry. He was angry because he felt he did everything in his power to remain faithful to a woman who had already lied and betrayed him in the worst way possible just to maintain her image with her family and her father's church. Donovan said to himself that he would have left Dominique for Nia had he known what he found out much sooner.

That was when the lightbulb came on. Donovan knew if Dominique were to find out that he cheated on her with Nia, it would crush her and she would hurt the way he was hurting. So Donovan's initial plan was to talk to Nia, tell her what happened and see if she would agree to his plan for getting back at her by having an affair. To Donovan's surprise, Nia agreed to everything he requested even though she knew she would be hurting one of her good friends who she still spent time with. It was evident that Nia still had feelings for Donovan and she was willing to take advantage of any opportunity presented to have him, even if it was only for sex. As Donovan and Nia continued talking about their plans to meeting up behind Dominique's back, Nia came up with an idea that blew Donovan's mind completely, but he liked it at the same time because it was going to really put the icing on the cake when it came to the amount of pain he would be able to cause his wife. It was Nia's idea to have his children and then ask Donovan and Dominique if they would be her children's godparents and make up a story about the children's father not being in their lives. After Judah was born, Donovan and Nia were both concerned that Dominique would be suspicious but she wasn't. She immediately said yes to being her children's godmother and their plan went into motion from there.

Donovan and Nia continued their affair, eventually having their other three children and giving all four of them Nia's last name instead of Donovan's; *Judah Timothy Westbrook, Joshua Isaiah Wesbrook, Joseph Michael Westbrook, and Justice Naomi Westbrook.* Donovan had always planned to give his children Biblical names or names with a spiritual purpose attached to it, so Nia allowed Donovan to name each other their children himself. Nia wasn't saved but she still allowed her children to go to church with Donovan every week and supported Judah when he stepped out a few months ago and started leading praise and worship.

Donovan was more nervous than he had ever been about his situation now that Ashleigh knew the truth about him being the father of his godchildren, and he wasn't sure if his threats would be enough to keep Ashleigh from talking. Yes, she did dance for a couple of months to pay for tuition and books, but no one would give that a second thought once it was made known that a prominent pastor in Atlanta had an ongoing affair with his wife's friend, intentionally had children with her and pretended that they were his godchildren. Donovan continued driving through the city not knowing what to do next. Donovan wasn't sure if Dominique had made it back home yet so he decided to stop in a shopping center nearby to call his mom to tell her what happened when he went to visit Ashleigh. Donovan was in a total panic as he talked to his mom about what happened and he was surprised to see how calm Leigh remained about the situation as he explained it to her. When she responded she asked Donovan if he was still at Ashleigh's place and he told her that he had already left before asking what he should do. Leigh sighed and paused for a moment before responding.

Leigh responded to Donovan by telling him not to worry and not to say anything to anyone about what happened because she was coming to Atlanta to talk to Ashleigh herself. Donovan froze after hearing the tone in his mother's voice when she made that statement because he knew it wasn't going to go well for Ashleigh, especially since Leigh was going to make a trip all the way to Atlanta just to talk to her. Leigh doesn't like to travel much so Donovan figured one of his other brothers would be with her when she came. Donovan agreed to do what Leigh told him and headed home shortly after ending his phone call with his mother. Donovan was relieved when he arrived home and Dominique hadn't arrived yet because it was going to give him a little more time to process what just happened before she got there. As Donovan sat on the sofa in the living room, he sent another text message to his mother and asked if she thought he should tell Nia what happened. Leigh took a moment to respond and when she did, she told Donovan not to mention it for now. Donovan knew Nia would be upset with him for not saying something when he first found out what Ashleigh did, but he still chose to do what his mom said. Moments later, Donovan is startled by his doorbell and hearing multiple knocks at his front door. He quickly got up and went to see who it was and was surprised when he saw Nia because she usually never comes to his house. Donovan didn't know why she was there and decided to come outside to talk to her since Dominique wasn't home yet.

"Nia, what are you doing here? Where are the kids?" Donovan asked, concerned.

"They're hanging out with their cousins at my dad's house. I needed to talk to you, Donovan!" Nia said in a panic.

"Nia, my wife isn't home and you being here without the kids doesn't look right at all. If Dominique pulls up and sees you, she's going to give me the third degree and I don't have time for it after the day I had after church!" Donovan said.

"Well you better hope she doesn't show up before I leave because we have much bigger problems!" Nia said as Donovan looked confused.

"What are you talking about, Nia? What's wrong?" he asked as the two of them walked over to where her truck was parked.

"I was at the store with our four children getting some food for the week and Justice saw your niece, Ashleigh and ran over to her. We walked over to speak to her and she gave me this look. I didn't like it so I had Judah take Justice and his brothers over to pick out some fruit while we talked." Nia said as Donovan shook his head in disbelief.

"I really don't like where this is going. Okay, what did Ashleigh say to you?" Donovan asked.

"She gives me this smirk and says "*Nia, you're smart but you're not smart enough.*" I asked her what she meant by that and that was when she told me that she knows that you're the biological father of Judah, Joshua, Joseph and Justice! Donovan Malik Hall, how the hell does your niece know that?" Nia asked, sternly as Donovan reacted to what she told him.

"Oh my God, I can't believe this is happening right now. I told her to keep her mouth shut!" Donovan said as Nia looked surprised.

"So you told your niece the truth? Why the hell would you do that?" Nia asked as Donovan attempted to calm her down.

"Nia, I know you're upset but calm down and stop talking so loud before someone hears you. You know good and well I wouldn't do that!" Donovan said.

"Then how does know and who else did she tell? Do you know this girl tried to ask me for money to keep quiet about it?" Nia asked as Donovan looked surprised.

"She asked you for money? How much?" he asked.

"She asked me for $50,000.00 to keep quiet and I of course told her where to put that $50,000.00! Now I know she's your niece but I told her that everyone in my family aren't doctors and lawyers. I have some cousins who will put her down and make her body untraceable if she really wants to mess with me." Nia said.

"You said that?" Donovan asked.

"Yeah, I said it. She walked away like she was unbothered but I could tell she was a little shook about it. Now tell me how she knows this! I don't want to call my cousins but I will if she ever tries me the way she did again!" Nia said.

"Nia, I just learned this today when I went to Ashleigh's house to ask her why she wasn't at church. That one day I left the kids with her and Malik when you were out of town, she had them tested because she had been suspicious for a while." Donovan told her as Nia reacted to what he told her.

"How did she even get your DNA?" Nia asked.

"I had something to drink before I left her place and she took the straw I used and the kids toothbrushes and had some friend of hers do the test." Donovan said.

"What friend, Donovan? I know every doctor in the city!" Nia said.

"She wouldn't tell me who it was. But there should be a way for you to find out, right?" Donovan asked.

"Yeah, I can look up the kids' information and it should show me something. There's going to be hell to pay for the person who did this. But the damage has already been done, Donovan. What do you plan to do?" Nia asked as Donovan sighed and paused for a moment before responding.

"Nia, you trust me don't you?" Donovan asked.

"Of course! That's why I came to you instead of calling my crazy cousins." Nia said as Donovan laughed a little.

"I don't want you to worry your pretty little head about Ashleigh or the fact that she found out the truth about me being the kids' father. I already have a plan in the works to handle that and I can assure you, she won't bring it up again nor will she blackmail you into paying her $50,000.00." Donovan said as Nia sighed in relief and nodded her head.

"Thank you, Donovan. Can you keep me in the loop?" she asked.

"Yes, I'll keep you posted but don't stress. I'm probably going to handle this and I'm sorry she came for you the way she did." Donovan said.

"Thank you. I'm just glad she didn't say it in front of the kids. I don't know how I would have explained that to them, especially Judah. I mean, I know one day the kids will know the truth whether we want them to or not but we should be able to tell them on our terms." Nia replied.

"Don't worry, Nia, we will! The kids won't have to know anything before time." Donovan said.

"So Ashleigh didn't ask you for money like she did me?" Nia asked.

"No, she didn't ask for money. She was acting as if she intended to cut me another way, but I got her together real fast!" Donovan said as Nia nodded.

"Okay, well she better watch her step before she ends up hurt for getting other people's business. I'll go ahead and leave before Dominique gets back." Nia said as she unlocked her car door and got inside.

"I'll call you this week and one of us will come pick the kids up Wednesday for Bible Study." Donovan said as Nia nodded and waived before driving away.

The next morning, Donovan ate breakfast with Dominique before she left to work a double shift at the hospital. She came home yesterday minutes after Nia left their house and he sighed in relief because he would not have gotten any rest had she come home and saw the two of them outside talking. Surprisingly Donovan had managed all these years to keep his relationship with Nia a secret and Dominique has never been suspicious of the two of them and his plan was to keep it that way by making sure Ashleigh didn't tell anyone what she knew. Leigh arrived late last night with Donovan's sister, Samantha who is Ashleigh and Malik's mother. Leigh told Samantha everything about Donovan's situation so she would have a better understanding of why they were making a random visit to Atlanta. Shortly after Dominique left for work, Donovan drove to his brother, Sebastian's house to meet Leigh, Samantha and Wesley to discuss their plans for confronting Ashleigh. Wesley and Sebastian weren't fully aware of Donovan's situation either so he decided to tell them everything including what he found out about him being a beneficiary on Dominique's father's life insurance policy. His family were in shock when he told them how much he would receive in the event that Dominique's father passed away and he went on to say that it was important that none of these secrets came out because if they did, Dominique's father would probably would remove him as a beneficiary and he would ultimately lose the church. As they were talking, Wesley asked Donovan if his plan was to keep all of this a secret for the rest of his life and he asked if his children would ever know the truth about who he really is.

Donovan really didn't know what to say to his brother's question. The truth was, Donovan had spent so much of his time making sure no one found out the truth that he never stopped to think about when the time would come to reveal what was hidden. Donovan replied to Wesley and said that as much as he hates to do it, he can't ever tell his kids the truth because things would change no matter what. Donovan said this not knowing that everything he's kept in the dark would have the light shine on it in a way that he would have never anticipated. He delegated roles to his family to help protect him in the event that something happened not knowing that even they would not be able to help him hide once everything came to the light.

"So you need all of us to handle Ashleigh?" Sebastian asked.

"No, you don't have to come with us for that. We will handle Ashleigh! We're actually going to her house after we leave here. I just wanted to bring you up to speed on everything and I wanted to ask you about Antoine Washington, too." Donovan said.

"Again? Donovan, we've already talked about this and we told you we made sure his body was dumped in a place that the police would never find it." Wesley said.

"I know, I just get nervous sometimes because after all these years, the police are still trying to investigate." Donovan said as Wesley and Sebastian glanced at each other.

"They still have him listed as an active missing person's case?" Wesley asked, surprised as Donovan nodded.

"Antoine's parents must have paid the department or something to keep investigating because it's still active. I saw a report about it last week." Donovan said.

"It's been almost fourteen years! They have to know by now he's not alive." Wesley said.

"I think they do know that part but they want to find the body and you know what will happen if they do. They will see that he was shot twice with my gun." Donovan replied.

"Bro, don't stress about it. They're not going to find his body. It's in a place that no one would think to look at, trust us!" Sebastian said as Donovan nodded.

After they finished their conversation, Leigh and Samantha left their truck parked at Sebastian's house so they could ride with Donovan to where Ashleigh stayed. Ashleigh didn't know Leigh and Samantha were in town nor did she know they were coming to see her so Donovan could only hope that she would actually be at her apartment when they got there. Donovan, Leigh and Samantha arrived at Ashleigh's apartment about fifteen minutes later. When they arrived, they saw Malik walking out from Ashleigh's building to his car talking on his cell phone. Leigh and Samantha quickly got out of Donovan's car and rushed over to speak to him before he left.

Malik ended his call in shock to see his mother and grandmother. Malik didn't know they were coming to town and he wondered why they were here, but he was still happy to see them. Malik was on his way to an appointment and couldn't talk long so he hugged Leigh and Samantha again and asked if he could see them again before they went back to Memphis. While Leigh and Samantha weren't here for a social visit, they promised to visit Malik before they got on the road. After Malik left in his car: Donovan, Samantha and Leigh started walking towards Ashleigh's apartment not knowing she wouldn't be alone when they got to her door. Donovan knocked and was surprised when his sister, Nichole answered the door and invited them inside as Ashleigh came out of the kitchen. Malik was rushing and forgot to tell them she was here.

"I had no idea you guys were in town! How are you?" Nichole asked as she hugged Leigh and Samantha.

"It was sort of a last minute trip, but we're okay. How are you doing?" Leigh asked.

"I'm great! I was in the area and decided to stop by and visit Ashleigh since I didn't see her yesterday." Nichole said as Ashleigh walked over to hug Leigh and Samantha.

"Grandma, you don't like to travel so you must be here for a reason." Ashleigh said, still confused by their sudden arrival at her apartment with Donovan.

"Yeah, you're right. I don't like to travel much and I am here for a reason, we're here to talk to you." Leigh said as Ashleigh glanced at Donovan who gave her a smirk while Nichole stood between them wondering what was going on.

"Is everything okay?" Nichole asked, concerned.

"Yeah Nichole, it's fine. We just need to talk to Ashleigh in private if you don't mind." Samantha said as Nichole glanced at Ashleigh who was doing her best to maintain her composure even though she was terrified.

"Well, we're all family and I don't want Ashleigh to feel alone so I think I should stay." Nichole said as Donovan shook his head.

"Nichole, we need to talk to Ashleigh alone."
Donovan replied as Nichole paused for a moment
before responding.

"Okay, I'm just going to be honest with
everyone. Something here isn't right and Ashleigh, I'm
picking you up in my spirit. You're not showing it but
you're terrified right now which makes no sense, but
it's why I want to stay to make sure everything is
okay." Nichole said as tears fell from Ashleigh's face.

"Nichole, we're fine and no offense but
Ashleigh is my daughter, so she's not scared! Isn't that
right, Ashleigh?" Samantha asked, glancing at
Ashleigh.

"Right..."

"See Nichole, we're fine. Stop trying to discern
us all the time just because Donovan made you one of
his fortune tellers!" Samantha said, sternly.

"Really, Samantha?" Donovan asked as Leigh
started laughing.

"I'm not a fortune teller, Samantha, I'm a
prophet! I'm a real prophet and if you won't tell me
what's going on, I know the Lord will!" Nichole said as
she glanced at Donovan.

"Nichole, I promise you we're fine. Let us talk
to her alone and we will try to catch up with you
later." Donovan said as Nichole sighed and glanced at
Ashleigh one more time.

"Ashleigh, are you okay with me leaving?"
Nichole asked as Ashleigh glanced at Donovan who
pointed to his gun on his waist.

"Yes ma'am, I'm fine. We just have some personal things to talk about so I'm okay. Thank you for coming to see me though, I appreciate it." Ashleigh said as she and Nichole hugged each other.

"Not a problem, Ashleigh. I love you and I'm going to miss seeing you lead worship at the church. But if Pastor Singleton's church is where God is leading you, I'll accept it for what it is." Nichole said as Ashleigh smiled and nodded.

"We will still get to hang out and I promise to come to the Summer Conference too." Ashleigh said.

"I can't wait! I'll call you later on but if you need me, don't hesitate to reach out." Nichole replied as she grabbed her things before walking out of Ashleigh's apartment.

"See you later, sis." Donovan said as Nichole hugged each of them.

"Okay guys, I love you. Mama, Sam, how long are you in town for?" Nichole asked as she walked to the door.

"We're probably going to leave on Friday." Leigh said as Nichole nodded.

"Call me before you leave." Nichole said.

"We will." Samantha replied as Nichole walked out of Ashleigh's apartment.

"Now I know you didn't go and open your big mouth to Nichole! You're already in enough trouble as it is!" Donovan said.

"Opened my mouth about what, Mama? I didn't even know Aunt Nichole was coming over. She just showed up." Ashleigh said, defensively as she wondered why they were there.

"I called them about our little conversation yesterday and they decided to assist me with paying you a visit because you apparently didn't take me seriously after we spoke." Donovan said, sternly.

"I did take you seriously!" Ashleigh said.

"No you didn't Ashleigh! You left my house, ran into Nia at the store and tried to blackmail her for $50,000.00 to keep quiet!" Donovan said, enraged as Ashleigh's expression changed. "What, you didn't think she was going to tell me? She showed up at my house in a panic because of what you said!"

"So you told Mom and Grandma?" Ashleigh asked.

"Yes, I told them, Wesley and Sebsastian about your little shenanigans." Donovan replied as Ashleigh shook her head.

"Why the hell did you tell them? You really must want me to talk!" Ashleigh said as Samantha abruptly slapped Ashleigh across her face causing her to fall on the floor.

"Mama, I can't believe you just slapped me!" Ashleigh said.

"First of all, you better not ever let me hear you speak to your uncle like that again after all he's done for you! Secondly, you're going to get more than that if you make us miss out on this money!" Samantha said, sternly as Ashleigh slowly picked herself up off the floor and sat in the chair at the dining room table.

"What are you talking about?" Ashleigh asked, confused.

"Ashleigh, you really should have minded your own business. I mean you had paternity tests done on your cousins because you were suspicious? Your uncle's affairs are none of your business!" Leigh told her.

"It is when I'm on his leadership team and he's not being integral." Ashleigh said.

"I thought you left your uncle's church." Leigh replied.

"I did! But this is a large part of why I left. I was suspicious and I couldn't help but feel that his godchildren were actually his kids! They're starting to look more and more like him, especially Judah!" Ashleigh said.

"You should have taken your suspicion to the grave and if you wanted to leave your uncle's church, so be it. We don't care anything about churches like that, we just care about the money." Leigh said.

"Yeah, and if Dominique finds out that he's the father of Nia's children, we're not going to get our cut of the money! I need that money and if you make us miss out on that by running your mouth, there will be hell to pay!" Samantha replied.

"What money are you talking about?" Ashleigh asked as Leigh and Samantha glanced at Donovan.

"Donovan, do you want to tell her what she got herself into by being so nosey?" Leigh asked.

"Dominique's father is getting older and I'm pretty sure that he won't be with us too much longer.

When he dies, I'm up for a big payday and I'm giving portions of it to Mama, Samantha, Wesley and Sebastian because they've helped me." Donovan said.

"So they've helped you keep the fact that you fathered four kids a secret?" Ashleigh asked.

"Yes, that's part of it." Donovan replied.

"So how are you getting paid by Aunt Dominique's father when he dies? You're on his life insurance policy or something?" she asked.

"That's right. I'm a beneficiary and I'll be a rich man once he goes. But if you talk, that will ruin everything. This is why you need to keep your mouth shut and pretend like none of this ever happened." Donovan said as Ashleigh paused for a moment before responding.

"How much are you getting?" Ashleigh asked as Leigh, Samantha and Donovan sighed in frustration.

"That's none of your business little girl!" Leigh said, sternly.

"Yeah, she's right. I'm not telling you that." Donovan replied.

"Well, I want a cut too!" Ashleigh said.

"What? I'm not giving you anything, Ashleigh!" Donovan said.

"You want me to keep your secret a secret right?" Ashleigh asked.

"You're going to keep this secret and you're still not getting any of this money!" Donovan said as Ashleigh started laughing.

"I don't know why you're laughing, Ashleigh, because we're serious!" Samantha said.

"Uncle Donovan only brought you guys here to try and scare me into staying quiet! I know what you're capable of but I'm family and I'm named after my own grandmother! You're not going to hurt me!" Ashleigh said as Donovan, Leigh and Samantha laughed sarcastically.

"That's where you're wrong baby girl. We can hurt you and we will if you don't get rid of your evidence and assure us that you won't say anything to anyone." Leigh said.

"Mama, is she serious?" Ashleigh asked, concerned.

"Yeah Ashleigh, she's serious and so are we. We don't want to hurt you, but you know how we are about money and we don't let anyone get in the way of that, not even family." Samantha said.

"I don't understand. How could you be helping Uncle Donovan cover this up when he's a pastor who's supposed to maintain integrity in front of people at all times? Isn't this why you've never gone to church and why you kept us from it?" Ashleigh asked as Leigh and Samantha glanced at each other.

"You're right Ashleigh, we do feel that way. We're not helping Donovan because we're in support of the church because we still hate it. This is strictly about the money and what we're going to get out of this!" Samantha said as Ashleigh shook her head in disbelief.

"We don't have all day, Ashleigh. Are you going to let us see you destroy the evidence you have?" Leigh asked.

"Yes, and promise that you won't speak about any of this to anyone?" Donovan asked.

After thinking about it for a few minutes, Ashleigh still wouldn't agree to Donovan, Leigh and Samantha's terms. She stood her ground in saying she wouldn't destroy the evidence she had and while she wasn't planning to say anything about Donovan's secret now, she couldn't promise that when the time was right she wouldn't reveal the truth unless they cut her in on the money that Donovan was guaranteed to receive as a settlement in the event that Dominique's father passed away. Donovan was not going to give her any of the money no matter what Ashleigh said to him so he, Leigh and Samantha did what they felt they had to do to keep Ashleigh quiet. They beat her up.

The three of them severely punched, slapped and kicked Ashleigh as she laid on the floor doing her best to cover face while she cried and screamed hysterically. They beat Ashleigh for nearly ten minutes and her screams eventually stopped when Donovan kicked her in the face so hard that it knocked her unconscious. Samantha turned Ashleigh on her back to see if she was still breathing while Leigh went into the kitchen and filled a pot full of cold water and came back over to where they were. Once Samantha confirmed she was still breathing, she and Donovan stepped back as Leigh poured the water on Ashleigh until she opened her eyes and started coughing.

"Do you still think we're playing?" Donovan asked as he knelt down beside her and she shook her head in fear as Leigh and Samantha stood behind him.

"Is this your phone?" Leigh asked, grabbing it off the table as Ashleigh nodded and coughed again.

"What did you store the evidence as? Are they photos?" Leigh asked.

"I just have screenshots that the person who did the test for me sent after it was done." Ashleigh said as Leigh handed the phone to Samantha.

"Find those screenshots and make sure they're deleted, please!" Leigh said as Samantha nodded.

"It's done! Now before you even think about calling your friend to send you more screenshots, we're already in the process of having him or her tracked down. I'm sure once they get fired and possibly even charged for what they did, they're not going to want to help you anymore." Samantha replied as Ashleigh's expression changed.

"How are you going to do that?" she asked.

"Don't worry about that, Ashleigh. Just know that you're not going to outsmart us and you better take this beatdown as your last and final warning!" Donovan said as Ashleigh started crying.

"We're leaving and you better not tell your aunt, Nichole or anyone else for that matter who did this to you or the next time you will get a nice little visit from your uncles! Wesley and Sebastian have already hidden one body, yours will be next if you talk! You got it?" Donovan asked as Ashleigh nodded.

"Baby, why did you make us do this to you? All you had to do was stay out of your uncle's business and you would not have even been on our radar. I raised you better than this, Ashleigh. You're starting to turn out just like your sisters and I'm over it at this point. Are you guys ready to go?" Samantha asked as they grabbed their things off the sofa.

"Yeah, let's get out of here. Hopefully no one heard her screaming and called the police." Donovan said as Leigh looked out the window to make sure there were no police cars outside.

"I don't see anyone so we should be good if we leave now." Leigh said as she quickly walked outside with Donovan and Samantha trailing behind her after closing the door to Ashleigh's apartment.

Donovan dropped Leigh and Samantha off at Sebastian's house where their truck was parked before heading to do some work at his office at the church. Donovan didn't express it to Leigh and Samantha but he was still worried about Ashleigh potentially saying something even though they did everything in their power to keep her silent. Donovan didn't want to draw any unnecessary attention to Nichole but he knew she didn't feel right about what was going on between them and it was why she was so reluctant about leaving Ashleigh's apartment when they asked her to. As Donovan continued driving to the church, he was hoping that Nichole went to work and didn't return to Ashleigh's apartment. He then started thinking about Malik and began to shake his head. He doesn't live too far from Ashleigh and they visit each other a lot, so he knew it wouldn't be long before he would pay Ashleigh a visit. But he was hoping he could stall and keep Malik from going over there for a while without coming across suspicious. As expected, Malik's car was parked outside when Donovan arrived at the church and he could hear Malik from outside playing the keyboard and rehearsing songs. Donovan went inside through the side door so that Malik wouldn't see him because he didn't want Malik to ask about Ashleigh while he came up with a plan to keep him from seeing her for a while. About ten minutes after Donovan was inside of his office, he heard a knock at the door and sighs because he knew it was Malik.

"Come on in, Malik." Donovan said as he continued typing on his computer.

"Hey Uncle Donovan, I didn't even see you come in." Malik said as he sat down in front of his desk.

"I came in through the side door and heard you rehearsing so I didn't bother you. How did you know I was here?" Donovan asked.

"I saw your truck when I ran out to my car to get something I left behind. Is my mom and Grandma still in town?" Malik asked.

"Yeah, they're still here. I dropped them off at your uncle, Sebastian's house before I came here to get some work done. You haven't seen your aunt around here have you?" Donovan asked.

"Aunt Nichole? No, I haven't seen her since I got ready to leave Ashleigh's house." Malik said.

"Yeah, about that. Why didn't you tell us Nichole was inside Ashleigh's apartment?" Donovan asked.

"Oh, I'm sorry. I was so excited to see Mom and Grandma, I forgot to mention it. Are they okay? They usually tell me when they're coming to visit." Malik replied.

"They're fine, it was last minute so they didn't get around to calling you. But I'm sure you will see them before they head back to Memphis." Donovan replied as Malik nodded.

"I talked to Uncle Brandon and Uncle Cam earlier. They seem to be okay but Uncle Brandon hasn't been the same since Bryan and Brenton died." Malik said as Donovan sighed and paused for a moment before responding.

"Yeah, you're right. Brandon doesn't do much of anything anymore outside of taking care of Bryson and Bryce. We keep telling him to get counseling and he won't go." Donovan said.

"I think I may have changed his mind about that." Malik said as Donovan looked surprised.

"Are you serious? How?" Donovan asked.

"Uncle Donovan, I know when you asked me how I was holding up with everything, I told you I was doing good. Part of why I was able to tell you that was because I went to counseling not long after I moved here for school." Malik said.

"I was wondering what you were doing to cope. So you went to counseling? That's good! Why didn't you tell me?" Donovan asked.

"I guess I never heard you say much about mental health and I didn't know how you were going to respond. But I had been having nightmares about the day we got shot and I couldn't get the images out of my head of Brenton and Bryan lying on the ground next to me not moving." Malik said as Donovan nodded.

"That was one of the scariest days of all of our lives. We were so relieved when we realized you were still alive and it crushed us when we realized your cousins weren't going to make it. I could only imagine the pain my brother was feeling after losing two of his sons and he really hasn't been the same since like you said." Donovan replied.

"Yeah, I know..."

"But you think he might finally go get help now? What did you say?" Donovan asked.

"I told him what I did for myself after everything happened and I even told him about God and how my relationship with him had been helping me stay strong." Malik said as Donovan nodded.

"That's good, Malik. So what did he say?" Donovan asked.

"He asked me to help him find counseling in Memphis and I told him I would look up some resources and send it to him. Even though he didn't officially say he was going to counseling, I figured that since he asked for help, finding a counselor was a start." Malik said.

"Yes, it's definitely a start and I definitely support his decision." Donovan replied as Malik nodded.

"Can I ask you something?" Malik asked.

"Sure, what's up?" Donovan asked.

"Why did my mom name me after you? I literally never asked about that before now." Malik said as Donovan laughed a little.

"Your mom never told you why she did it?" Donovan asked, surprised.

"No, I don't remember her doing it." Malik replied.

"Well, this will sound odd but your mom decided to name you after me because we were at my birthday party when she found out she was pregnant with you." Donovan said as Malik reacted to what he said.

"Are you serious?" he asked.

"Yes, I'm serious! I can't believe she never told you. But yes, we were at my birthday party and we were scared because Samantha suddenly passed out in the backyard. Someone was going to call an ambulance but your grandma decided to drive her to the hospital herself." Donovan said.

"Wow, so that was the end of your birthday party?" Malik asked.

"Yeah, the party was pretty much over after that and I didn't care, I just wanted my sister to be okay. When we got there, the doctors ran tests and they asked her if there was any chance she was pregnant and she said she wasn't. But then she found out she was and later on when she found out when she found out she was having a boy, she looked at me and said she was naming him after me and that we would call him Malik." Donovan said.

"Oh wow, that is so crazy. I had no idea it happened like that." Malik replied as Donovan smiled a little.

"Yeah, I still remember it like it was yesterday. I used to wonder what would happen when I had my own son and I wanted to name him after me but you see the situation I'm in. So naming you after me worked out better than I expected it to." Donovan told him as Malik nodded.

"Can I ask you something else?" Malik asked as Donovan laughed a little.

"You can ask me anything, Malik. What's going on?" Donovan asked.

"Was I right about Ashleigh? Did she take Pastor Singleton's offer?" Malik asked as Donovan nodded and took a sip of his water.

"Yes, you were correct. That was exactly what she did." Donovan replied as Malik shook his head.

"I can't believe she jumped ship like that. Uncle Donovan, do you think she's jealous of me?" Malik asked, concerned as Donovan paused for a moment before answering his question.

"I don't think she's jealous, I think she just felt left out and wanted something for herself." Donovan replied as Malik nodded.

"I know you didn't want her to leave the church but you don't think it's a big deal that she went to Pastor Singleton's church do you?" Malik asked.

"Yes, it is a big deal. Like I told you, Cedric has been bitter ever since Dr. Ellis turned him down and didn't allow him to take over the Atlanta location." Donovan said.

"So Pastor Singleton targeted us hoping we would leave and come over to his church?" Malik asked.

"Yeah, that was pretty much it. He was going to feel like he won and got revenge by taking my two best singers who happen to be my niece and nephew." Donovan replied as Malik nodded.

"Well, I hope Ashleigh thinks it was worth it. I'm not leaving, I'll always be here for you." Malik said as he and Donovan slapped hands.

"I appreciate that, Malik and that's why you're as blessed as you are." Donovan told him.

"Ashleigh must be mad at me or something." Malik said as Donovan's expression changed.

"Why do you say that?" he asked.

"I've texted her like three times and I called her once. She's still not responding. I'll probably just go over there on my way home." Malik said as Donovan almost panicked.

"Well, you don't have to do that. She won't be home. She got ready to leave not long after we came by to see her." Donovan said.

"Really? Did she say where she was going?" Malik asked.

"We're not really sure but she had an overnight bag so maybe Cedric got her a gig somewhere or something." Donovan said.

"It can't be that, she would have told us about it. You said she had an overnight bag packed?" Malik asked, confused.

"Yeah, she said she was going to take care of something and would be back in a couple of days and that was it. So she probably won't be home if you go over there." Donovan said.

"But she's not answering my calls or replying to my messages." Malik replied, concerned.

"She's probably still on the road, Malik. Don't worry, she'll call you back once she's settled. Just give her some time." Donovan said.

"Okay, I'll wait until tonight to see if she calls me back. If she doesn't, I'm going over there in case she comes back early or something." Malik said as Donovan tried to quickly come up with something that would keep Malik from going over to Ashleigh's apartment.

"What are you doing tonight besides tracking down your sister?" Donovan asked.

"I'm free tonight, what's going on?" Malik asked.

"Do you remember Pastor Jones? His church is in Marietta." Donovan said.

"Oh yeah, I remember him. His two daughters have that food truck right?" Malik asked.

"Yes, that's right! He texted me a moment ago and said his musician had something come up tonight and can't play for the first night of their revival and he needs a last minute replacement. Can I send you over there?" Donovan asked as Malik thought for a moment.

"I have to go all the way to Marietta just to play the keyboard for one night?" Malik asked.

"Well, Pastor Jones plans to make it worth your while. There's a thousand dollars for you if you go." Donovan said with a smirk as Malik reacted to what he said.

"A thousand dollars to play the keyboard for one night? Are you serious?" Malik asked, surprised.

"Oh yeah, Pastor Jones' money is very long. If he says he's paying you a thousand, he means it. So can I tell him you're coming?" Donovan asked as Malik started nodding and Donovan laughed at him.

"Okay, good. I'll let him know you will be there and I'll text you the flier with the address. The service starts at seven but I think the church will be open well before that time so you can get there early." Donovan said.

"Oh yeah, I'm in! I remember his set up so I won't even need my keyboard. He has everything over there!" Malik said as Donovan started laughing again.

"Yeah, he does." Donovan replied.

"Alright Uncle Donovan, thanks for the gig! I'm about to go lay down a while before tonight so I'll probably see you tomorrow." Malik said as he and Donovan hugged each other.

"Okay Malik, no problem. I'll talk to you later. I love you." Donovan replied as Malik got ready to leave his office.

"I love you too." Malik replied.

Donovan sighed in relief after Malik walked out of his office because he hoped having Donovan get ready to play the keyboard at this other pastor's service tonight would keep him from going to Ashleigh's house. Donovan knew he, Leigh and Samantha hurt Ashleigh pretty badly and he couldn't help but wonder what she would do to treat her injuries. He knew if she went to the doctor or to the hospital, they would call the police and if Ashleigh talked, it would expose everything Donovan had been keeping a secret from his church, his wife and the rest of the world. Nichole is married with four sons of her own so Donovan expected for his sister to go straight home once she left work, so that left Ashleigh's new church. Donovan wasn't sure when Ashleigh would be expected back there again and he didn't think about the fact that she can't show her face there until her injuries heal. Donovan saw how afraid Ashleigh was as they left her apartment so he didn't expect her to talk no matter what happened next.

Moments later he received a text message from Nia who said she was outside of the church with their children who were asking to see him. Donovan

quickly headed outside to the front entrance where
Nia was parked to see them. Judah, Joshua, Joseph
and Justice jumped out of Nia's truck and ran over to
hug Donovan and tell him about their day. Donovan
grabbed his things, locked up the church and decided
to treat Nia and the kids to lunch at the kids' favorite
restaurant so they could spend more time together.
After they finished eating, they went to a park that
had a large playground and basketball court. Judah
saw some of his friends from school on the court and
he ran over to play basketball with them while
Joshua, Joseph and Justice walked over to the
playground. Donovan and Nia sat at a picnic table
near where the kids were playing to talk while they
watched them.

"Donovan, thank you for taking time to spend
with the kids today. They were so excited." Nia said as
Donovan nodded.
"You're welcome, anything for my kids."
Donovan replied.
"I can tell something's wrong, Donovan. Did
your mom and your sister make it to town yet?" Nia
asked.
"Yeah, they're here. We were together earlier
today." Donovan replied.
"Oh okay, that's good. If they want to see the
kids before they leave, let me know." Nia said.
"I will.."
"So did you get a chance to talk to Ashleigh
again?" Nia asked as Donovan sighed and paused for a
moment before responding.

"Yeah, the three of us went to her apartment this morning to confront her about what she said to you and everything else too. We almost had a problem when we got there though." Donovan said.

"What was the problem?" Nia asked.

"My sister, Nichole was at her apartment when we got there and you know how she is. She's too discerning sometimes and when we got there, she was getting this weird vibe and she was acting like she wasn't going to leave at first." Donovan said.

"That's not good. I'm assuming she left at some point, right?" Nia asked.

"Yeah, she left but she looked at us like she knew something was up even though she didn't know what it was." Donovan said.

"Nichole is the one you said is a prophet, right?" Nia asked.

"Yes!"

"Is she always accurate?" Nia asked.

"Yes!"

"Wow, okay. Well, I hope she doesn't walk up to you one day and read you like a book, Donovan." Nia replied.

"You and I both! But I'm more concerned about what will happen if she goes back to Ashleigh's today or within the next week or so." Donovan said.

"Oh no, did you guys beat Ashleigh up?" Nia asked.

"I didn't want to hurt my own niece but this girl was not going to back down. She wanted the money I'm getting when Dr. Ellis dies!" Donovan said as Nia reacted to what he told him.

"Are you serious?" Nia asked.

"Yeah! I'm not sure what she needs all this money for but she was acting like we owed her something because of what she knew. Then she thought she wouldn't be in danger because we're related but I let her know she wasn't exempt." Donovan said.

"How bad did you guys beat her?" Nia asked as Donovan shook his head.

"It was pretty bad, Nia. She was unconscious for a minute but we made sure she was awake and alert again before we left her apartment. I just hope her neighbors didn't hear her screaming and called the police or anything." Donovan said.

"Wow Donovan, I knew you were planning to keep her quiet, but I didn't know you would go that far on your own niece." Nia said.

"So you're judging me now?" Donovan asked.

"Of course not, Donovan. I'm just saying. If she was knocked unconscious, you really must have hurt her. She probably needs to see a doctor!" Nia replied.

"Yeah, she probably does but she's not going to if she knows what's good for her." Donovan said.

"Donovan, she's going to need medical attention. I know I haven't seen her but I'm sure her injuries won't be taken care of with just bandaids and alcohol." Nia replied.

"Okay, so what do you want me to do about it? You know if she sees a doctor, they're going to call the police. Ashleigh probably won't talk but still, the police can't be anywhere on our radar if we want this plan to work out." Donovan said.

"Do you think Nichole is going to go back to her apartment today?" Nia asked.

"I don't think so. She has a family of her own so she'll probably head home after work but I won't be surprised if she doesn't call her." Donovan replied.

"What about Malik?" Nia asked.

"He has a gig tonight, he's not going to see her, at least not today and possibly tomorrow." Donovan said as Nia sighed and thought for a moment before responding.

"Where are we at with Dr. Ellis? Is he any closer to checking on out of here so we can get paid?" Nia asked.

"He has his days where he's okay, but it won't be long from now. I won't be surprised if he isn't gone by the Summer Conference." Donovan said as Nia nodded and continued watching their kids.

"I know I shouldn't even care right now after what your niece did but what if I go over to her apartment and treat her wounds." Nia said as Donovan's expression changed.

"You will do that for real after how she came at you?" Donovan asked.

"Yeah, I will if she will let me. I can't have anything getting in the way of that money and we both know she won't be able to hide in her apartment forever. I mean, doesn't she have a job?" Nia asked.

"Yeah, she works at a call center but she took some time off this week. I don't think she will go back until maybe next Tuesday." Donovan replied as Nia nodded.

"Well, she needs to be as healed as possible before then or else someone will see her and the wrong people are going to start asking questions." Nia said.

"Yeah Nia, you're right about that." Donovan said.

"Okay then, it's settled. When we leave here, I'll take the kids to my dad's house, I'll grab my medical kit and head to Ashleigh's apartment. Just text me the address." Nia said.

"Alright, I will. Thank you. You don't have to do this but I appreciate it." Donovan said.

"It's all good. I don't want to miss out on my cut either and if this comes out, you already know your wife's father won't be giving you anything." Nia said.

"Yeah and I'll be in danger." Donovan said as Nia's expression changed.


"What do you mean?" she asked as Donovan sighed.

"You think my family has been helping me for free? My mom, my sister and my brothers are expecting their cut, especially my brothers. They hid an entire body for me! So yeah, a lot is riding on Dr. Ellis' death and me getting this money." Donovan said.

"Wait a minute, Donovan. Are you saying that if something happened and you didn't get this money to pay them, they would come after you?" Nia asked, still shocked by his response.

"Yes, my brothers will kill me. That was the agreement." Donovan replied as Nia shook her head.

"That is so crazy. Well on that note, let's go. It's been an hour so that was enough time." Nia said as she and Donovan stood and walked over to where Joshua, Joseph and Justice were playing.

"Let me go get Judah off the court, I'll meet you at the truck in a minute." Donovan replied.

"Okay..."

"Nia, I know we always said the kids would never know the truth about me being their father but I've changed my mind." Donovan said.

"You have?" Nia asked.

"Yes, we can tell them once I have the money because I'll have enough to walk away from the church and do my own thing." Donovan replied.

"That's fine, but what if things don't go as planned." Nia said as Donovan paused for a moment before responding.

"If anything happens and I don't get the money, tell the kids right away and do your best to explain it to them. I don't mind trying but I probably won't be around for much longer if I don't end up getting this money so make sure the kids always know how much I love them and how much I appreciate you for giving me what my wife couldn't." Donovan said as Nia did her best not to start crying.

"Do you mean that, Donovan? I know you love the kids, but do you appreciate me for real?" she asked.

"Yes, yes I do! I know this situation wasn't ideal and it wasn't right but you understood what I needed and that my wife doing what she did prevented me from being able to have what I always wanted, which was the opportunity to be a father." Donovan said as Nia smiled a little and nodded.

"Well, you're welcome. In a way, we both got what we wanted." Nia said as Donovan laughed a little.

"Yeah, I should have been with you when I had the chance but I thought Dominique was it for me." Donovan replied.

"It's okay, we all make mistakes. But it's not too late to correct the mistake either." Nia said with a smirk.

"Well, let me get paid first and we can talk about it." Donovan replied.

Donovan and Nia's plan for her to treat Ashleigh's wounds so that people wouldn't know that she was assaulted fell through when Nia went to Ashleigh's apartment and she didn't come to the door. Nia initially assumed that Ashleigh wasn't home but Donovan described the kind of car she had and Nia saw that it was still parked outside of her building. Nia left once it was clear that Ashleigh wasn't going to come to the door and she drove to her father's her house to pick up her their kids while Donovan sat in his home office wondering if Ashleigh was actually home and just didn't come to the door for Nia, or if she left with someone. Donovan was going to call his mom and sister to discuss it more with them until Nia sent him a message saying that she was taking the kids over to Sebastian's house so that Leigh and Samantha could see them. Donovan decided to wait. Moments later Dominique called him to check-in and they talked for about a half-hour before he got off the phone with her and he remained at his desk thinking about everything that had been happening so far. Donovan didn't want to admit it to anyone but deep down he knew the walls were really starting to close in on him and that his time of his secrets being in the dark would soon be coming to an end.

A couple of hours later while Donovan had dozed off on the sofa inside of his office, he heard his cell phone ring from his desk and he slowly got up from the sofa as it stopped ringing and then started again. It was Dominique calling him and he saw the text message she sent telling him to answer his phone because it was urgent. Donovan answered Dominique's call as he took a sip of water and almost dropped his glass when Dominique explained why she was calling him again. She told Donovan to come to the hospital because Ashleigh was there being treated for several severe injuries from an assault. Donovan asked Dominique before getting off the phone with her how Ashleigh arrived at the hospital and he shook his head when Dominique told him that it was Nichole and came in with Ashleigh. Donovan quickly ended his call with Dominique and called

Leigh and Samantha to tell them what happened and where he was headed.

Leigh and Samantha wanted to come with him and at first, Donovan didn't think it was a good idea until Wesley suggested that he take them because the police will want to ask them questions if Nichole tells them that they were the last people she saw with Ashleigh earlier today. Even though Dominique never said that the police were called, he figured they would be notified because of the severity of Ashleigh's injuries and there would be a good chance that Nichole would tell them the last people she saw with Ashleigh were him, Leigh and Samantha. Donovan knew he couldn't ask Nichole not to tell the police that information because it would only make him look more guilty and even more suspicious to Nichole. Donovan drove in a panic to Sebstain's house to pick up Leigh and Samantha before heading to the hospital. On the ride there, they started rehearsing their stories and planning out what they would say to the police in the event they were questioned about Ashleigh's injuries. They were more worried about Ashleigh breaking down and telling them the truth about everything, which would ultimately ruin everything and Donovan wouldn't get the payout he had been promising his family for helping him out all of this time.

As Donovan pulled into the parking lot of the hospital, he received a call from Sebastian with more news. Nia found out the name of the nurse who Ashleigh paid to complete the paternity test. They weren't working at the hospital tonight and Nia was able to find their address and give it to them so they could pay the person a visit. After Sebastian finished telling Donovan the rest of their plans with paying this nurse a visit at her home, they ended their call and Donovan agreed to follow up with them sometime tomorrow once the job was done. Donovan called Dominique to let her know he was at the hospital as he, Leigh and Samantha walked through the front entrance and waited near one of the elevators for Dominique to meet them. The first elevator opened and Dominique held the door as she signaled for the three of them to get on with her and head to the sixth floor where Ashleigh was being treated for her injuries. The hospital didn't waste any time because as Donovan, Leigh and Samantha walked into Ashleigh's room, there was a police officer inside taking Ashleigh's statement as Nichole sat at her bedside while Dominique stood nearby and looked over her chart. As she reviewed Ashleigh's stats, Dominique couldn't help but notice the strange vibe between Ashleigh, Nichole, Donovan, Leigh and Samantha when they arrived. It became even stranger when Donovan, Leigh and Samantha spoke to Ashleigh and asked if she was okay and she barely said two words to them.

"Hello, are you more of Ashleigh's family?" the officer asked.

"Yes, I'm her uncle, Pastor Donovan Hall and this is her grandmother, Leigh Hall and her mother, Samantha Hall." Donovan replied as the officer greeted each of them.

"I'm Officer Ron Walker with the Atlanta Police Department, and I was just getting Ashleigh's statement. I'm glad you guys are here though, I was going to reach out to you next because I feel like there's something missing in this story." Officer Walker said as he glanced back at Ashleigh who was doing her best to maintain her composure.

"So you don't believe me?" Ashleigh asked.

"I'm not saying that, I'm just saying I feel like you're holding back on me and I don't know why. Just like I'm not sure why it took your aunt dropping by your apartment and seeing your injuries hours after you were assaulted before you got help. It's almost as if you weren't planning to say anything at all." Officer Walker said.

"It's not like that." Ashleigh said, shyly as Nichole continued holding Ashleigh's hand.

"Nicole here said that she came to Ashleigh's apartment earlier today and she wasn't injured like she is right now. I asked her if she was the last one to see her before her assault and she told me the three of you were inside of Ashleigh's apartment when she got ready to leave around eleven this morning. Is that true?" Officer Walker asked.

"Yes, Nichole saw us at Ashleigh's apartment before she left but she can't confirm that we were the last ones with her so I'm not sure why she's saying this to you as if we had something to do with her attack!" Leigh said, sternly as Nichole glanced back at them and shook her head.

"No one's being accused, I'm just trying to get to the bottom of what happened to your family member." Officer Walker replied as he made more notes on his tablet.

"Ashleigh baby, it's okay to tell the officer what really happened. You're safe and I won't let anything else happen to you." Nichole said as she tried to fight back tears.

"I told him what happened. I was attacked when I was walking the back trail to the store." Ashleigh said as Nichole sighed and shook her head.

"Ashleigh, you know that's not true. Tell him what really happened." Nichole pleaded.

"Nichole, did you see Ashleigh get attacked?" Officer Walker asked as Donovan, Leigh and Samantha glanced at her.

"No sir, I didn't but I know this attack wasn't random and it didn't happen the way Ashleigh is describing it. She's covering up for someone, I feel it!" Nichole replied, sternly.

"Is that true, Ashleigh?" Officer Walker asked as Ashleigh shook her head.

"Officer, I know they called you but I'm not pressing charges and I'm not making a report." Ashleigh said as tears fell from her face and Donovan nodded slightly while Dominique stood nearby hearing the entire conversation.

"So this attack on the trail with a black man in a dark hoodie isn't true is it?" Officer Walker asked.

"No sir, it's not and I'm sorry!" Ashleigh said as she broke down and Nichole rushed to hug her.

"It's okay Ashleigh, I'm not upset with you. I just wanted you to confirm that so I wouldn't document this. So you don't want to tell me what really happened so we can make an arrest? These injuries you sustained could have killed you, you know that right?" Officer Walker asked.

"Yes sir, I know but it's safer for me not to talk than it is for me to say anything at all. Believe me!" Ashleigh replied as she cried more.

"Officer, can I please tell you what I think?" Nichole asked.

"You can, but if you don't have proof or if it isn't something you witnessed, I can't do much." Officer Walker.

"I understand but you need to look closer at my brother, Donovan. I think he did it and if my mom and my sister were promised something in return, they probably helped him!" Nichole said in a stern tone as Officer Walker's expression changed.

"Wait a minute, you're accusing your brother, your mother and your sister of hurting Ashleigh? That is a big reach for someone who didn't see anything. Why would you make such an accusation?" Officer Walker asked as he calmed Donovan, Leigh and Samantha down who were reacting to what she said.

"Ashleigh was one of Donovan's main praise and worship leaders at his church and she left recently to go to a rival leader's church here in the city. I knew Donovan would be bitter about it but I didn't think he would take it this far!" Nichole said.

"Are you kidding me right now, Nichole? Beat the crap out of my niece because she went to a new church? You're crazy!" Donovan said, defensively.

"Well if what your sister is saying is true, it could give you a motive. Did Ashleigh actually leave your church recently to be the praise and worship leader at another church?" Officer Walker asked as Donovan shook his head.

"I can't believe this! Yes, she did but I didn't care! I had her brother, Malik and my godson, Judah to lead in her place so it's not like she was stopping anything by leaving!" Donovan said.

"Yeah but she left without telling you ahead of time and she went to Cedric Peterson's church and everyone knows how feels about you since Dr. Ellis gave you the church instead of him!" Nichole said.

"Officer, ignore everything that my aunt just said because it wasn't like that. No, I didn't tell my uncle I was leaving but that was only because everything happened so fast. Uncle Donovan and I talked and we're fine. Aunt Nichole, you really need to let this go." Ashleigh said as Nichole looked confused.

"Ashleigh, that's not what you told me when I came to see you. You said Donovan was furious!" Nichole replied.

"No, I didn't. You misunderstood me. Officer, there's nothing here for you to investigate. I'm not talking. Once I get treated, I'm going home and I'm going on with my life and that's it!" Ashleigh said as Nichole shook her head in disappointment.

"Baby, you don't have to do this!" Nichole said.

"Aunt Nichole, I'm fine!" Ashleigh replied.

"Alright, if Ashleigh isn't going to back up what you're saying and she's not going to give an official statement then there's nothing I can do. She can call the precinct at this number on the card if she changes her mind." Officer Walker said, handing a card to Nichole before walking out of the hospital room.

"Nichole, what the hell? Why would you throw your own mother, brother and sister under the bus like that for something you know they didn't do!" Dominique said, walking over to where they were standing.

"First Lady, I'm sorry but I wouldn't say it if it wasn't true! I knew I felt something in my spirit wasn't right when they all showed up at Ashleigh's apartment and I should have stuck to my guns and stayed behind. They did this and with all due respect, First Lady, you need to open your eyes!" Nichole said.

"What are you talking about?" Dominique asked as Nichole grabbed her purse and started walking towards the door.

"I'm saying stop pretending like your woman's intuition hasn't been kicking at you like crazy! Maybe neither of us have all the details but Donovan is not as integral as he claims!" Nichole said.

"What?" Dominique asked.

"Sis, you need to watch your mouth! I'm still your pastor!" Donovan said as Nichole turned around.

"Not anymore and as far as I'm concerned, you're not even my brother!" Nichole replied, angrily.

"Hold on a minute, Nichole Marie Hall-Pearce! You can't be talking to your brother or to any of us like that!" Leigh said.

"Mama, Donovan is up to something and he's been up to it for years. I just don't know what it is, at least not yet. See pretty soon, we will all know the truth and when it comes out, you won't be able to beat us up like you did Ashleigh to keep us quiet!" Nichole said.

"You don't know what you're talking about? Do you know how crazy you sound right now accusing us of hurting our own blood?" Samantha asked.

"I'll be the crazy one if that's what it takes but soon all will see that I was right! Donovan, I don't know what Ashleigh found out about you but whatever it was, was going to ruin you and your ministry and you couldn't let that happen. So you came to her apartment to confront her about it and you were caught off guard when you saw me, all of you were. Now I don't know what Mom and Sam have to do with any of this, if anything they're just getting some kind of pay out of it and my spirit tells me you've dragged Wesley and Sebastian into your mess too!" Nichole said as Donovan, Leigh and Samantha started laughing.

"Nichole, go home to your husband and get some rest. You're obviously tired!" Leigh replied.

"Hold on a minute Nichole, if you're going to bring this drama you can stay away from our church and take your family with you!" Dominique said as Nichole laughed sarcastically.

"Wow First Lady, you really don't have a clue. That's fine, I don't want to be a part of your church when it all comes to the light anyway so consider me gone! All I know is Donovan did something really bad and he's spent the last several years trying to cover his tracks so no one, especially you, finds out the truth. But all of that is about to change and everything he's been trying to hide is going to come out! My prayer now is for Ashleigh to speak up because she knows, she knows it all. You won't admit but you know who assaulted you, Ashleigh. They're right here. You told them what you knew and you threatened to expose your uncle and when you wouldn't promise him that you would keep quiet, they beat you up so you would be too afraid to say anything! I know I'm right, that's why you're crying! But baby you don't have to suffer in silence and you don't have to be afraid of your uncle because he has a title! His title is not bigger than God and you don't have to be afraid to speak, Ashleigh! The enemy won't have your voice! Ashleigh, I'm going home for a bit but if you still need me to pick you up when you're discharged, you can call me and you can stay with us if you want." Nichole said as Ashleigh nodded.

"I love you Aunt Nichole, thank you. I'll let you know." Ashleigh replied as Nichole nodded and walked out of the room.

"Dr. Hall, we have a gunshot victim that was just brought in by ambulance!" a nurse said to Dominique who quickly laid down Ashleigh's chart and walked out of the room to assist.

"Wow Ashleigh, you're tougher than I thought you were. Good job." Donovan said, walking over to her as Samantha and Leigh stood on the opposite side of her bed.

"Okay fine, you see I didn't talk. Can you guys just go?" Ashleigh asked as she wiped her face with the tissue she had in front of her.

"Yeah, we can go..."

"Hold on Donovan, how do we know she didn't talk to Nichole! I mean she almost came out with everything just now!" Samantha said.

"Samantha, you know our sister is a prophet. She's always been able to see and discern everything, you know that. If really knew everything, she would have said it in front of the officer." Donovan said as Samantha nodded.

"Look, I won't talk, okay? I just want you guys to leave me alone and never talk to me again! I hate you!" Ashleigh said as tears fell from her face.

"Ashleigh, you don't mean that." Leigh said.

"Are you serious? Look at my face! Look what you guys did to my body! I hate you!" Ashleigh said.

"Girl, you better quiet down! Now listen, we didn't want to hurt you but you were the one acting all bold and threatening to expose your uncle!" Samantha said.

"Yeah Ashleigh, you left us no choice! You wouldn't even be involved had you not gone behind my back and had my kids tested. That's where you messed up and now you and your secret friend you

didn't want us to know about is going to pay for it."
Donovan said as Ashleigh looked confused.

"What are you talking about?" she asked.

"You weren't going to tell me who had that test done for you thinking I wouldn't find out, but I did." Donovan replied.

"No, no way!" Ashleigh said as she shook her head.

"I found out who it was, Ashleigh. You forget Nia is a doctor too and can look things up. She put Judah's name in the system and just that fast, she found the paternity test that was done and the name of the nurse who did it. What was her name? Oh yeah, Kenya!" Donovan said, laughing sarcastically as Ashleigh started crying and begging them not to hurt her.

"Uncle Donovan please, she needed the money and I pushed her to do it! It wasn't her fault, it was mine! Please don't hurt my friend! She has a husband and four kids of her own." Ashleigh pleaded as she started to panic.

"Yeah Ashleigh, you're a little too late. I already sent my brothers to her house." Donovan replied as Ashleigh broke down in tears.

Donovan looked at his phone and saw that Wesley and Sebastian had tried calling him three times but he missed the calls because of the signal inside the hospital. Donovan, Leigh and Samantha decided to leave and Donovan called his brothers back as they got on the elevator and headed to their car in the parking lot. Donovan was expecting his brothers to tell him that they killed Kenya and got rid of her body but they told him a different story. When they arrived at Kenya's house, they broke in once they saw that she was alone and everything was going as planned until they saw headlights outside and realized her husband had come back home sooner than they thought he would. Wesley went on to explain that he shot Kenya in the chest before running out the back door and through the woods leading out to a different street that was near the area where they parked their truck. Donovan panicked as he drove as fast as he could to Wesley's house with Leigh in the passenger seat and Samantha in the backseat. Wesley and Sebastian were just getting home when Donovan, Leigh and Samantha arrived.

"Bro, start from the beginning and tell me what happened when you went to Kenya's house?" Donovan asked as they went inside and sat in the living room while Samantha grabbed wine for everyone to drink.
"Sebastian and I pulled up and saw that her boyfriend and the kids were all home. We initially thought we were going to wait until they went to bed to break in, tie up the boyfriend and kill the girl. But the boyfriend ended up leaving and the way he was dressed, it looked like he might be gone for a while." Wesley said.
"So about ten minutes after he left, we parked our truck on a different street in a wooded area where no one could see us and we walked the trail

leading up to her house. We broke in and Kenya started screaming while all of her kids ran to the back room. We asked her for the results of the paternity test like you asked us to and she wouldn't give them up!" Sebastian said as Donovan shook his head.

"Wait a minute! Donovan, you had them ask for the results instead of just killing her? What if one of the kids heard you say it or something and tell the police, then what?" Leigh asked, sternly.

"Mama, I'm sorry but one dead body is enough and I was trying to avoid having my brothers dump another one. All I really needed was the file so I told them to get it from her and only kill her if she refused to give it up." Donovan said as Leigh shook her head while pouring more wine into her glass.

"I get it but I still would have just shot her. What's one more body?" Leigh asked as Donovan said.

"Guys, continue. What happened after that?" Donovan asked.

"The girl's boyfriend suddenly came back and we panicked when we saw his lights outside the window. We shot Kenya in the chest when she started screaming again and we ran out the back door through the kitchen and we left." Wesley replied.

"So you don't know if she's dead or alive right now, right?" Donovan asked.

"Right, we were long gone before that. I mean, more than likely her boyfriend called the police and the ambulance or whatever." Wesley said.

"You better hope she died on scene because if she didn't, she's going to tell the police what you said and it won't be long before they connect the dots." Leigh said.

"That's not necessarily true, Mama. Think about it, she would have to tell the police that she conducted an unauthorized paternity test with her employee login and computer. If she lived, I'm sure she wouldn't want to lose her job by confessing to what she did." Donovan said.

"I guess I didn't think about it, that's true. But what about Ashleigh? She's going to find out about this and it could break her silence." Leigh replied.

"No it won't. You saw how things went at the hospital tonight, if she wanted to talk, she would have done it then." Donovan replied as Leigh nodded.

"Yeah, that's true. Nichole was trying to make Ashleigh talk to that officer but she didn't break." Samantha said as Wesley and Sebastian glanced at each other.

"Nichole was at the hospital?" Welsey asked.

"Yes, she was there and so was Dominique. Nichole must have gone by Ashleigh's apartment sometime after Nia left and she saw her injuries and took her to the hospital where my wife works." Donovan said.

"So Dominique heard everything you guys said? Did she ask you about it?" Sebastian asked.

"No, but that was only because she got called out of the room to an emergency. But I'm sure she will be after everything Nichole said." Donovan replied.

"So she knows what's going on?" Wesley asked.

"No, but she's being so suspicious and discerning about everything, you might as well say she does." Donovan said.

"Please don't tell me we have to go after our own sister about this." Sebastian said.

"We're not going after her, she doesn't know anything and being suspicious doesn't hold up in court." Donovan told them as they all nodded.

"Donovan this plan of yours is starting to unravel and you're nowhere near getting your money which means we're nowhere near getting our cut!" Wesley said, sternly.

"You're going to get your money, Wesley! Stop worrying!" Donovan replied.

"Are you serious right now? We're one confession away from being arrested and thrown in prison for the rest of our lives and we don't even have what you said we would get for helping you!" Wesley replied.

"Maybe you should go find Nia and tell your kids the truth about who you are before you die." Sebastian said.

"Boys, calm down." Leigh said.

"No way, Mama! Do you know what all we've done to help *the pastor* keep his church and keep his reputation?" Sebastian asked, sternly.

"I know, but he's still your brother. No Mama, he's our half-brother and a deal is a deal. Donovan knows what is going to happen if we don't get our money." Sebastian said as he and Wesley stared at him.

"Guys, it's not going to come to that. You're going to get your money." Donovan said.

"How can you promise that when your wife's dad is still alive and you're on the verge of being exposed and taking all of us down with you?" Wesley asked, enraged.

"I don't know for sure but I have to hope, that's all I have left at this point." Donovan replied.

"Listen Donovan, we really don't want to kill you and take you from your kids. I mean at least your kids actually like you, our exes turned our kids against us a long time ago!" Wesley said.

"So what are you saying? You won't hurt me if this falls through?" Donovan asked.

"That depends on how well you can help us if we do get busted. Pay for our defense lawyers to get us off and we won't come after you." Sebastian replied as Donovan's expression changed.

"Really? That's it?" Donovan asked.

"Yeah, if you can pull that off." Wesley told him.

"I have connections with several defense lawyers so don't worry. If it comes to that, I'll be able to get the best one that money can buy, trust me." Donovan said.

"Let's just focus on what we have going on right this moment and hope that no one starts talking at this point." Samantha replied as everyone agreed with her.

"Donovan, let me ask you something. What was the conversation between you and Dominique's father when he decided to make you a beneficiary on his life insurance policy?" Leigh asked.

"There was no conversation, he never told me. As a matter of fact, we still to this day have never talked about it." Donovan said as Leigh, Samantha, Wesley and Sebastian looked surprised.

"Okay, wait a minute, Donovan. If you guys never talked about it, then how do you know you're listed as a beneficiary on his policy?" Samantha asked, confused.

"I found out a long time ago when I was home one day while Dominique was out shopping at the mall. She had a copy of the policy sitting on her desk when I went in there to look for something I needed and I looked through it. I wasn't expecting to find anything and then I got to like page forty and there it was." Donovan said as his family glanced at each other, still shocked by what he told them.

"Dominique has never said anything to you either?" Wesley asked.

"No, not once! It made me think that she must not know either. See I know how Dominique is, she doesn't like reading through stuff all the way so she probably didn't read to page forty. Her mom and her sisters never said anything to me either so I honestly believe that he added me and didn't tell them because I know Dominique and her sisters always felt like their dad liked me more than them because he never had a son." Donovan said.

"Oh wow, Dominique felt like that and still chose to be with you?" Leigh asked as Donovan shrugged.

"Yeah, she did but as you can see, I wasted my time. I should have left her for Nia when I had the chance." Donovan replied.

"Nia went to college with you guys, right?" Samantha asked.

"Yeah, that's right." Donovan said.

"Nia was the friend that Dominique told her secret to about the real reason she couldn't have kids?" Samantha asked.

"No, it wasn't Nia. She told another friend of hers who lives in Virginia now. They were talking on the phone and I overheard them." Donovan said.

"I might as well say it, Donovan. I don't know how no one was suspicious before now to be honest with you. I mean, the kids look just like you in their own way." Sebastian replied.

"Yeah, that's true. The older they get, the more they look like me, especially Judah." Donovan said.

"Yeah, Judah is the spitting image of you when you were thirteen. I would have known he was my grandson even if you had never come to me about it." Leigh said as Donovan laughed a little.

"Man, we should just leave town now before anything happens!" Wesley said.

"Trust me, I want to! But we need to stay around until the police question us. In the meantime, we need to come up with a story that sounds consistent so that they won't catch us in a lie. Once we're cleared as suspects, we can go as far as we need to go and Donovan can send us the money he owes us whenever his father-in-law takes his last breath." Leigh told them.

"You're right, it won't look good if we skip town. So wait, you and Sam are staying too?" Wesley asked.

"Yeah, we're going to hang around a while until this passes. Brandon, Cam and the kids should be fine until we get back. It's crazy, they don't know about any of this." Leigh said.

"Well you know Brandon hasn't been the same since his sons were killed and Cam became a whole family man once he had his kids. He would never do this with us now." Sebastian said.


"So your kids are still not letting you talk to them?" Donovan asked as Wesley and Sebastian shook their heads.

"Not at all. They really act like they don't want anything to do with us and their moms won't let us see them." Sebastian replied.

"Are they still in West Palm Beach?" Donovan asked.

"Yeah, last we checked." Wesley replied.

"Have you ever just gone out there to see them?" Donovan asked.

"We tried that once and their crazy moms almost called the cops on us. We didn't try it again after that." Wesley said as Leigh reacted to what he said.

"You didn't tell me that, Wesley." Leigh replied.

"I know, Mama and I'm sorry. I just didn't want you to get too upset and do something crazy." Wesley replied.

"All this money and we're still empty. I need to get some sleep, I have meetings with two clients tomorrow." Sebastian replied.

"Yeah, so do I. Keep us posted on things, Donovan. Mama, Sam, you guys can stay here as long as you need to." Wesley said.

"Thanks guys, we appreciate it." Samantha replied as Donovan's phone went off and he grabbed it to see who the message was from.

"Is everything okay, Donovan?" Leigh asked, noticing Donovan's expression change.

"I don't think so." Donovan said as he sat staring at his phone.

"What is it?" Samantha asked, concerned as Donovan started to grab his things.

"Dominique just sent me a message and said that if I was still with you guys, we needed to meet her at the police headquarters downtown." Donovan said as everyone glanced at each other.

"Are you serious?" Wesley asked as Donovan showed him the message.

"The police station? What the hell's going on? That girl must have died! Is there anything on the news about it?" Wesley asked as Sebastian, Samantha and Leigh checked the news station reports on their phones.

"We don't see anything. This is crazy. So much for getting some sleep. Let's go, guys." Leigh said as they grabbed their things and left the house.

Wesley volunteered to drive everyone in his truck this time to the station. Donovan called Nia to tell him what was going on and to see if she knew anything, but before he could she called him saying that she had to drop their children off at her father's house because she got the same text from Dominique saying she needed to come to the police station. But she didn't give any details on why they needed to meet her there. Donovan and Dominique didn't talk long at that moment but they both knew it was possible that Dominique knew everything about their secret and everything else that had taken place as well. As they rode to the station and were quickly trying to come up with their story for the police, Donovan called Nia back to let her know what they were planning to say so she would make sure her story matched theirs in the event they were questioned separately.

When Donovan and his family walked into the front lobby of the station, he saw Dominique in tears as she stood and spoke to two detectives near the admin's desk. Nia walked into the station not long after they did and Dominique pointed them out to the detectives who immediately turned around and walked over to talk to them as Dominique introduced each person. None of them knew what was going on and were doing their best to maintain their composure until they heard what the detectives had to say. Donovan knew something was really wrong when Dominique gave him a look of disgust and refused to hug him or hold his hand as they walked to the back of the station where the interrogation rooms were located. As they continued following the detectives, Donovan glanced over and saw Ashleigh, Nichole and Nichole's husband, Ryan sitting in one of the interview rooms talking to a detective. Ashleigh was crying more hysterically than she was before and he couldn't help but worry that she was possibly telling them everything she knew, which wouldn't look good for them.

Donovan was placed into an interrogation room by himself while they divided Dominique and the rest of his family into individual rooms where they would be interviewed by a detective one on one. Donovan had never been so nervous in his life and he wondered if he should just ask for a lawyer or give his statement to the detective who had stepped out and left him in the room alone. Donovan started receiving text messages from Malik who was trying to figure out what was going on. He was just now leaving the church he played at tonight and he only knew that Ashleigh asked him to come to the station because she needed to tell him something. Donovan sighed and shook his head when he read the message. Donovan replied to Malik and told him that they were all at the station getting questioned about something but he didn't know what it was. He went to tell Malik that no matter what happened, he loved him and he was sorry. Malik was confused and replied back asking for him to explain, but the detective entered the room and Donovan knew he needed to focus. He quickly responded back to Malik again and said he couldn't talk anymore and explained that he would eventually see what he meant by his statement before putting his phone on silent.

"Hey Pastor Hall, did you need water or anything before we get started?" the detective asked.
"I have some water in my bag, I'm fine. Can you tell me what this is about and why you called all of us down here at almost one in the morning?" Donovan asked, sternly as the detective laughed sarcastically.
"I find it funny that you really want to sit here and pretend like you don't know what's going on." he said.
"I don't!" Donovan replied, sternly.
"But you do. You just didn't think anyone would find out your secret since you're this big popular pastor in the city." the detective said with a smirk.
"What are you talking about?" Donovan asked.
"Wow, you're really going to play dumb with me, Pastor Hall? My son was right about you." the detective said as Donovan's expression changed.
"What are you talking about?" he asked.
"You remember Officer Walker, don't you?" he asked.
"That's your son?" Donovan asked, surprised.

"Yeah, he's my first born. I think you might know something about that don't you, Pastor Hall?" he asked.

"What?" Donovan asked as the detective started laughing again.

"I'm Detective Charles Walker, Sr. You can call me Detective Walker. Earlier this evening, my son came to see me after a very odd interview and encounter he had with you, your mom, Ashleigh Hall who goes by Leigh, your sister, Samantha Hall and your niece, Ashleigh Hall who I can see is named after her grandmother. Samantha is Ashleigh's mother correct?" Detective Walker asked.

"Yes..."

"Yeah, he came to me and gave me your name in particular. He said there could be a potential scandal at work here and to keep an eye out for anything that may come about after explaining what took place when he went to interview your niece who suddenly recanted when you, Leigh and Samantha showed up." Detective Walker said as Donovan sighed and shook his head.

"Okay, but you work for homicide. Why would he give you our names? I haven't killed anyone!" Donovan said.

"Are you sure about that, Pastor? My sources tell me differently." Detective Walker said.

"What sources? What are you talking about?" Donovan asked as Detective Walker paused for a moment before responding.

"We will get to all of that in a moment. Are you ready to begin this interview?" Detective Walker asked.

"Yeah..."

"Does this girl look familiar to you?" Detective Walker asked, showing Donovan a picture of a young woman.

"No, I don't know her." Donovan said.

"Her name was Kenya Reece. Does it ring a bell now?" he asked as Donovan shook his head.

"No it doesn't, I don't know her." Donovan said.

"Well Pastor Hall, she knew you and she even said your name seconds before she died after getting shot in the chest earlier tonight. You wouldn't happen to know anything about that would you, Pastor Hall?" Detective Walker asked.

"No, I don't!" Donovan said, sternly.

"Okay, this dumb game you're playing is going to land you in prison for the rest of your life! So since you want to act like you have this case of amnesia, I'm going to help you out and I'll see if you still want to play with me after that." Detective Walker said.

"Whatever." Donovan replied as he leaned back in his seat.

"While we were at Kenya's house investigating the shooting, Kenya was in the hospital fighting for her life after being shot in the chest right in front of her children!" Detective Walker said, sternly.

"I don't know what you're talking about." Donovan said as Detective Walker paused for a moment before responding.

"While we were investigating, we received a phone call and guess who it was from?" Detective Walker asked.

"Who?" Donovan asked.

"Your wife..."

"My wife had your number?" Donovan asked.

"Yeah, she does and that's because I'm at the hospital investigating one shooting after the next. So I see Dr. Hall pretty often." Detective Walker said.

"Okay, fine. So why did she call you tonight?" Donovan asked.

"She called me because right before Kenya died, she told her boyfriend that if anything happened to her, tell the police to talk to your niece, Ashleigh, who I later learned was a good friend of hers. Her boyfriend asked her why and Kenya told him that it was her fault that she had been shot. He didn't understand so he asked her what she meant and that was when she said Ashleigh paid Kenya to do a paternity test on her four cousins because she wanted to see if they belonged to you and she called you by name. She told her boyfriend that the kids she had tested are yours and she took her last breath after that." Detective Walker said as Donovan was left speechless.

"I can't believe she said all of that." Donovan said.

"Well believe it because she said it. Kenya's boyfriend told your wife what she said." Detective Walker said with a smirk as Donovan shook his head in disbelief.

"No, please tell me he didn't do that. He said
that to my wife?" Donovan asked.

"Yeah, he did. He didn't know that was your
wife until later, he thought he was only talking to the
doctor who was treating his girlfriend. He had no idea
he was exposing you to your own wife. Ashleigh had
not been discharged yet from the hospital so she held
off on her release until we arrived so we could get the
full story from Ashleigh." Detective Walker said.

"So you went and talked to my niece at the
hospital?" Donovan asked.

"Yeah, I did and then we brought her here. In
case you're wondering, she told us everything. She
didn't hold back like she did when my son tried to
interview her. She was done covering for you when
she realized she lost her friend because of what she
had her do. Ashleigh felt guilty and she felt like she
owed it to Kenya's family to tell us what she knew so
you can sit here all you want and act like you don't
know what's going on, but Ashleigh told us
everything. You might as well come clean now."
Detective Walker said as another detective knocked
on the door and walked in with Dominique behind
him.

"What is it?" Detective Walker asked,
wondering why they came inside.

"I know this is not how we typically do our
interviews but Dr. Hall insisted on speaking to her
husband alone for a bit before we continued. I figured
we could make an exception for her since we know

her from the hospital." the detective said as Detective Walker sighed and glanced at Donovan.

"Okay, we can give them a moment to talk." Detective Walker replied as he grabbed his things before walking out of the interrogation room.

"Hey, baby!" Donovan said as Dominique sat across from him still in tears.

"Don't speak to me, Donovan! I really can't even stand to look at you right now, but I want answers after the punch to the stomach I took tonight finding out that my husband deliberately had an affair with my good friend and got her pregnant! I knew you were upset that we weren't going to be able to have children together, but I had no idea you took it this far! How could you?" Dominique asked, disgusted as Donovan reacted to what she said.

"I should be asking you that, Dominique!" Donovan replied, defensively as Dominique's expression changed.

"What are you talking about?" she asked.

"I heard what you said to Cindy not long after we got married and found out you were barren. You told her about your little secret that you conveniently decided not to tell me about." Donovan said, enraged.

"Oh my God, you heard what I said to Cindy?" Dominique asked, surprised.

"Yes, I heard every word! After all that trash you talked about waiting until marriage, you cheated on me! Now I heard it was more than one guy but the one who counts most to me is Antoine Washington because he's part of the reason why you got pregnant

and had an abortion our senior year of high school!"
Donovan said as Dominique shook her head.

"My dad would have killed me if I told him I
was pregnant. I couldn't let that happen so I did what
I had to do!" Dominique said.

"You should have told me! What part of that
don't you get?" Donovan asked.

"Would you have married me had I told you
beforehand?" Dominique asked.

"No, I would not have married you," he said.

"Yeah, you would have gone running to Nia,
right?i That's who you really wanted, isn't it?"
Dominique asked.

"No, I wanted you! But you lied to me
Dominique, you lied to everyone so don't sit up here
and act like you're some kind of saint! All of this
happened because of you!" Donovan said as
Dominique laughed sarcastically.

"Donovan, I may have been wrong for not
telling you the truth about why I was barren but this
stunt you pulled is on you and not me! I haven't even
had a chance to tell my parents what you've done
because I'm still trying to wrap my mind around it all!
Our godchildren are your kids and you've known that
all these years! Nia has gone to lunch with me,
conferences, dinner, movies and all kind of things
pretending to be my friend while she had sex with my
husband and gave him the one thing I couldn't!"
Dominique said as she took a deep breath and started
crying again.

"All I care about right now is how I'm going to break this news to the kids. I mean, Joseph and Justice will be a little confused but they won't give me a hard time. I'm more worried about Judah and Joshua because they're older." Donovan said.

"You can cross that bridge when you get to it, we have bigger fish to fry. The Summer Conference is literally in a month and we're about to have one of the biggest scandals ever to hit Atlanta and it involves our church! Do you know how much we're going to lose now?" Dominique asked.

"We can find a way to keep the press out of this, Dominique." Donovan said as Dominique started laughing sarcastically.

"Donovan I know you're not that stupid! A girl is dead because you had her killed when Nia looked up the information about the test and told you who Ashleigh paid to have the kids tested. Now Ashleigh may have overstepped her bounds doing what she did, but it was for the best!" Dominique said as Donovan's expression changed.

"How can you say that?" Donovan asked.

"Donovan, you weren't going to say anything! You were just going to go on and carry this to the grave had none of this come out! I mean did you really think you could have four children with another woman and keep it a secret for the rest of your life?" Dominique asked.

"I was doing just fine with it until Ashleigh decided to become a private investigator." Donovan said.

"Donovan, who did you pay to kill this girl that died tonight?" Dominique asked.

"I didn't go after her, Dominique!" Donovan said.

"Donovan Malik Hall, stop it! You did and the police have a witness statement!" Dominique said.

"You're talking about what Kenya told her boyfriend before she died?" Donovan asked.

"No, I'm talking about Kenya's 10-year-old son who watched and heard everything. He told the police that the two men dressed in black with masks kept asking for test results. So you still want to play this game, Donovan? Who the hell did you pay to go after her?" Dominique asked.

"I didn't send anyone to go after Kenya." Donovan said.

"You're getting on my nerves! So what about Antoine?" she asked.

"What about him?" Donovan asked.

"Did you kill him because you found out we slept together and I got pregnant by him? I mean, no one else had an issue with Antoine deep enough to kill him. You're the only one with motive after overhearing what I said to Cindy!" Dominique said.

"No, I didn't kill Antoine." Donovan said.

"You're lying!" Dominique replied.

"Okay, prove it!" Donovan said as Dominique's expression changed.

"Did you really just say that? People who make those types of statements know they're guilty and refuse to admit it." Dominique said.

"That's your opinion." Donovan said.

"And what is this I hear about you my dad having you listed as a beneficiary on his life insurance policy? That detective must have you confused because Dad never told us that." Dominique said.

"I was wondering if he ever did because he never talked to me either, but I am listed. Look at page forty and you will see it." Donovan said.

"Well, I'm sure he's going to change that once I get done talking to him." Dominique replied as the detectives walked back into the room.

"No he's not. I'm the son he always wanted and he won't drop me no matter what you say." Donovan replied as Dominique got up from her seat.

"Can I go home now, please?" Dominique asked as Detective Walker sat down after she got up.

"Ronnie, can she go? She's not a suspect." Detective Walker said as the other detective nodded.

"Get your stuff out of my house as soon as they let you go! If I see any of it when I wake up, I will put it outside and I'm changing every lock so don't bother trying to stay!" Dominique said to Donovan as she stormed out of the room with the other detective leaving him and Detective Walker to talk alone.

"Did you record our conversation?" Donovan asked.

"Of course we did and you know that, that's why you wouldn't tell your wife the truth. But I'm glad we let you two talk because I'll need to call my friends at the Memphis Police Department about their cold case for your high school buddy, Antoine Washington." Detective Walker said.

"She's lying, I didn't kill him!" Donovan said.

"I don't know if I believe that. I looked up that case while you were talking and it's like your wife said, no one had any reason to kill him. No one except for you. But Memphis Police will question you about that I'm sure. Right now, we need to focus on Kenya Reece and the fact that your brothers just asked for lawyers." Detective Walker said with a smirk as Donovan's expression changed.

"What? They asked for a lawyer? Why?" Donovan asked, surprised.

"Well, they denied everything just like you until we told them we were going to get a warrant from the judge that would allow us access to their phone records and the tracking information on their car. Even if they used a burner phone, the information from their truck wouldn't lie and there are cameras all throughout the neighborhood that Kenya and her family lived in." Detective Walker replied as Donovan shook his head.

"It is?" Donovan asked, surprised as Detective Walker nodded.

"Yeah, it is and it won't be long before we have the footage we need to show who was at Kenya Reece's house the night she died." Detective Walker said.

"Whatever, am I under arrest?" Donovan asked.

"Yeah, you are. But it's not for Kenya's murder, not yet anyway. Ashleigh told us about the assault at her apartment. You, your mother and your sister beat the crap out of her from what she tells us." Detective Walker said.

"She can't prove that we did anything. We came to her place to say hello and then we left. We don't know what happened after that." Donovan said.

"Donovan, stop the games! Ashleigh told us how angry you were when she confronted you and told you that she was leaving your church after finding out that your godchildren are actually your kids. She told us how she tried bribing the kids' mother, Nia Westbrook. She told us how she threatened to expose you if you didn't give her a cut of some insurance money you were entitled to receive as a beneficiary on your father-in-law's policy in the event that he dies." Detective Walker said.

"Okay fine, all of that is true but we didn't hurt her!" Donovan replied, defensively.

"Yes you did! You wanted her to keep your secret so that it wouldn't ruin your reputation as a pastor. She refused to promise that and she refused to tell you who did the test so you beat her! Then you had Nia research and find out who the nurse was that administered the test and that was how you found out about Kenya. I think you sent your brothers to kill Kenya and your family has been helping you live this twisted double life for one reason and one reason only. You more than likely promised them a cut from the money once you received it if they helped you.

Dr. Hall told us how sick her father is, so you're expecting that money to come any moment now and that's assuming he doesn't remove you once Dr. Hall tells him what you're being accused of." Detective Walker told him as Donovan shook his head.

"He's not going to remove me no matter what happens, trust me!" Donovan replied.

"How can you be so sure?" Detective Walker asked.

"I just know!" Donovan said.

"Well Pastor Hall, I can't arrest you tonight but I will arrest you very soon once we get what we need. So I suggest you follow your brothers' lead and get your attorney too because you're going to need it!" Detective Walker told him.

Donovan, Leigh, Samantha, Wesley and Sebastian were released from custody from the time being because the police didn't have enough to make an arrest. The five of them drove back to Wesley's house to talk about what their plan of action would be next. When they arrived, Donovan was going to leave and head home to get his things before Dominique changed the locks but he was more concerned about getting caught and having everything he's worked to keep a secret come to light. As they sat inside the house, Donovan tried calling Nia because she left the police station before they did. He started to worry when she wasn't answering her phone so he kept trying, but he still wasn't getting an answer so he sent several text messages. Nia still wasn't responding.


"What's wrong, Donovan?" Leigh asked.

"Nia's not answering her phone or responding to my messages." Donovan said.

"It's almost three in the morning, Donovan. She's probably asleep since the kids are at her dad's house." Samantha said as she started yawning.

"I'm sorry but something doesn't feel right, I think something is wrong and I'm going to check on her. Anyone want to come with me?" Donovan asked as he grabbed his keys and started towards the door.

"Wait a minute, Donovan. We need to think about this first. What if something is actually wrong? The police are already on our backs, we don't need more drama!" Leigh said as Donovan stopped at the door and sighed.

"I get that and you're right. Listen, let's just ride over there at least. If Nia's cars are outside and if everything seems peaceful, we can just come back and I'll call her again in the morning once she's up." Donovan said.

"You really think something is wrong, don't you?" Samantha asked as Donovan nodded.

"Yeah, I do. Dominique was supposed to go back to work for another four hours and when she left the police station, she told them she was going home and I just didn't feel right about it. She knows everything now and I'm sure she's just as angry at Nia as she is at me. I just want to make sure she didn't do anything stupid." Donovan said.

"Oh wow, I didn't think about that. Does Dominique own a gun?" Leigh asked as they left the house and got into Donovan's truck.

"No, but I know my second gun is in my safe at the house and Dominique knows the combination." Donovan said as he quickly backed out of the driveway and started down the street.

"You really think your wife is capable of hurting someone?" Sebastian asked.

"I don't put anything past anyone, you know that. This is personal for her. If Nia was anyone else, she probably would be more focused on attacking me then the woman but Nia has been friends with Dominique since our freshman year of college. The last fourteen years have been a lie in more ways than one and the more Dominique thinks on that, the angrier I believe she will get." Donovan said as he continued driving.

Fifteen minutes later as Donovan got closer to where Nia lived, he saw the flashing lights from several police cars, a firetruck and an ambulance. Donovan turned onto Nia's street and realized at that moment that his suspicion was possibly right when he saw all of the first responders outside of Nia's house. Donovan quickly parked on the side of the street a few feet away from Nia's house, quickly got out and started running towards Nia's house as Wesley and Sebastian ran behind him. Samantha and Leigh quickly got out as well and walked as fast as

they could to Nia's house. As Donovan, Wesley and
Sebastian got to the front yard, they were stopped by
several officers who wouldn't let them go inside.
Donovan explained that this was his children's
mother's home and he wanted to make sure they
were okay and find out what happened. One of the
officers asked them to wait and said they would have
one of the detectives come speak with them because
no one else could go inside the house now that it was
officially a crime scene. Donovan looked over and saw
a large white homicide van parked near the
ambulance and he looked to his right and saw
Dominique's car parked in the driveway behind Nia's
truck and he knew something was terribly wrong.

"Well look at this, you guys just saved me a trip
to your house." Detective Walker said as Leigh and
Samantha walked up to where Donovan, Sebastian
and Wesley were standing.
"What are you doing here, Detective?"
Donovan asked.
"I was going to ask you the same thing, Pastor
Hall." Detective Walker said, glancing at all of them.
"When we left the station, the front desk lady
said that Nia left a half-hour ago so I called to check
on her and to make sure the kids were good, even
though I knew she had dropped them off at her dad's
house before she went to the station." Donovan said
as Detective Walker sighed and nodded before
responding.
"Okay, I'll just tell you the truth. A 9-1-1 call
came through from a neighbor across the street who

said she heard two gunshots from inside Ms. Westbrook's house. Initially, they dispatched two squad cars to the house and when they got here, it was totally dark inside the house. The police were going to leave until one of the officers realized the front door was slightly opened. They drew their weapons and went inside. They walked through the house checking every room and then they got to Nia's room." Detective Walker said as tears fell from Donovan's face.

"Just tell me what happened to her, please." Donovan said as Sebastian placed his arm around him.

"I'm sorry to tell you this but we found Ms. Westbrook in her bed with a single gunshot wound to the head. She was already deceased by the time we discovered her." Detective Walker said as Donovan broke down as his family tried to calm him down and comfort him.

"Detective, do you know who did it? Did the suspect leave?" Leigh asked as they helped Donovan gather himself so he could hear what the detective said next.

"We know who did it but they shot themselves in the head right after they killed Ms. Westbrook. That person was also deceased inside the bedroom on the floor when we found them." Detective Walker said.

"Who did it?" Donovan asked as Detective Walker sighed again before responding.

"Pastor Hall I'm sorry but it was your wife, Dr. Dominique Hall. She did it. She shot Ms. Westbrook before turning the weapon on herself." Detective Hall said as Donovan shook his head and more tears fell from his face as his family stood close to him.

"Was the gun a revolver?" Donovan asked as Detective Walker's expression changed.

"That's exactly what it was, how did you know?" Detective Walker asked.

"That's my other gun that I kept in a safe and I have the permit for it if you need it. I can't believe Dominique killed Nia with my gun! She must have taken it with her before she went to Nia's house. That was the real reason I came over here to check on Nia. I knew how mad Dominique was when she left the station and I knew something wasn't right when she said she was going home instead of going back to work at the hospital. She never misses a day." Donovan said.

"Detective, my grandkids weren't inside were they?" Leigh asked, concerned.

"No ma'am, there were no children inside, thankfully. Pastor Hall, you said they were at their grandfather's house?" Detective Walker asked as he took notes.

"Yeah, Nia took them to her dad's house. His house is about another fifteen minutes from here. Did you call him yet?" Donovan asked as a large van from one of the local news stations pulled up to the scene.

"We were going to wait and go see Dr. Westbrook and tell him in person but we're going to have to call him now before they start reporting. I'll be back to talk to you guys in a minute." Detective Walker said.

"Wait a minute, what about Dominique's parents and her sisters? They live in Memphis." Donovan said as Detective Walker thought for a moment before responding.

"I wasn't going to tell you this yet after what you just found out but I might as well. Right before the call came in about the shots fired, an officer was on their way to your house to see if your wife was home because her family was trying to reach her too and she wasn't answering her phone." Detective Walker said.

"Do you know why they were trying so hard to reach her?" Donovan asked.

"No, they didn't tell me why but I have to call one of my friends in Memphis to notify Dr. Hall's family about her death. Can you write their names here for me real quick?" Detective Walker asked as Donovan quickly did what he asked.

Moments after Detective Walker walked away from them, Donovan looked at his messages and saw several missed calls, voicemails and text messages from Dominique's family, his sister, Nichole, Malik and other members and leaders from his church. One of the messages said that Dominique's father had just passed away. Donovan was in total shock and he didn't know how to respond because none of them were aware that Dominique had just murdered somone and taken her own life afterwards. But

Donovan knew they were going to soon find out when he saw the news anchor reporting what was happening on a live recording. Donovan quickly sent a group text message to Dominique's family and everyone from the church to make them aware of what happened to Dominique and he apologized in advance for the text by explaining that he was doing his best to give them a heads up because the news media already started reporting what happened before the police could notify next of kin.

"Bro, I know this might not be the right moment but it looks like we're still going to get our money doesn't it? I mean, I don't think he knew the truth about what you did." Wesley said.

"Yeah, he didn't know. I'm probably going to wait and file my claim once they do the reading of the will, whenever that is. This is crazy though, I don't know what's about to happen." Donovan said.

"It's too bad we didn't come straight here from the police station, we probably could have stopped Dominique from killing Nia." Samantha said as Donovan nodded.

"That's what I was thinking. The kids are going to be devastated. I need to go see them and tell Dr. Westbrook and the kids myself." Donovan said.

"Okay man, let's go. Detective Walker knows how to reach us if he needs to. Let's get out of here, I'll drive and we can head there now." Wesley replied as they quickly started walking down the sidewalk where the truck was parked as more police and other people started to arrive on scene.

# SIX MONTHS LATER

It's been six months since the murder of 30-year-old, Kenya Reece and the murder-suicide of 37-year-old, Dr. Dominique Ellis-Hall & 37-year-old Dr. Nia Westbrook. The police were able to gather the evidence they needed to arrest and charge Wesley Hall and Sebastian Hall for Kenya's murder. Both brothers were each sentenced to seventy-five years with no possibility for parole. Leigh and Samantha were charged with a felony for the assault of Ashleigh Hall and were each sentenced to three years in prison with five years of probation. Donovan would have been charged as an accessory in their murders and additionaly charged for the premeditated murder of Antoine Washington, but he tragically comitted suicide by hanging himself inside of his bedroom before the arrest could be made. A month after Dominique's father, Dr. Shawn Ellis died, Donovan was invited to the reading of his will where it was revealed to Dominique's mother and two sisters that he would receive a million dollars as a sole beneficiary on his life insurance policy.

Even though Dominique's sisters wanted to dispute their father's decision after everything that was exposed with the church and Donovan's actions, the decision Dr. Ellis remained in place because he was competent at the time that he listed Donovan on the paperwork several years prior when Donovan was 13-years-old. Dominique's sisters were devastated by learning that their father left the majority of his money to Donovan when they were only related by way of his marriage to Dominique. They assumed it had to do with the fact that Dr. Ellis always wanted a son but never had one, but they soon learned that Dr. Ellis' reasons for the decision were from a place of secrecy, guilt and shame. There was a part to Dr. Ellis' will that was sealed and not permitted to be opened by his estate representative until after he passed away. The representative opened the document at the reading and it was at that time that Donovan found out a dark truth that was worse than anything he could have ever done or kept hidden from anyone. The letter that was handwritten and signed by Dr. Ellis stated that he was Donovan's biological father. He secretly had him tested the first month they met after meeting Donovan's mother because she looked familiar to him. Dr. Ellis went on to explain in the letter that when the test came back saying that Donovan was his son, he realized that Donovan was a result of his own dark past.

In the letter. Dr. Ellis admitted to raping Donovan's mother while she was a prostitute. They were supposed to meet for sex at a hotel and when she arrived, she changed her mind about having sex with him and tried to leave. Dr. Ellis went on to explain that he was heavily intoxicated at the time and became extremely angry with Leigh for trying to leave and he grabbed her before she walked out of the door. He slapped her repeatedly until she was unconscious and then he brutally raped her. When she came to, he gave her the $100.00 she asked for and sent her out the door and threatened to kill her if she told anyone what happened. Years later, Dr. Ellis got saved, married and started his own church and his own family thinking he could put his past behind him. But his past showed up the day he met Donovan and realized that Leigh not only got pregnant by him raping her, but she didn't choose to terminate the pregnancy. He left the one million dollars to Donovan out of guilt for what he did because he knew he would never find the courage to tell him the truth because he would have to own his part in what he did to his mother. Donovan had a nervous breakdown and completely lost it after the letter was read because he realized that if Dr. Ellis was his father, that meant he had been married to his half-sister for the last fourteen years and no one ever told either of them the truth.

Donovan tried talking to his mother about what happened and she couldn't take it. She cried and she kept apologizing but she wasn't ready to tell Donovan about what happened with her being raped, getting pregnant with him and having no clue who the father was because the didn't know the real name of the man she slept with him. She never saw him again so she didn't realize that Dr. Ellis was the man who raped her and got her pregnant the day they met and she allowed Donovan to be mentored by him. Donovan wanted answers and even after what he had just experienced and learned, she still wouldn't tell him everything so he could find some level of closure and peace of mind. Donovan killed himself the day that the money from the life insurance policy was deposited into his bank account.

Before he died, he left a signed letter apologizing to his four children, his nephew, Malik, his niece Ashleigh and everyone else who ever cared about him for what he was about to do. The last part of the letter requested for the money he received from the insurance policy to be dispersed among his four children into a trust that each of them could receive when they turned eighteen. Donovan's children; Judah, Joshua, Joseph and Justice were now living in North Carolina and were permanently in the care of their uncle, Pastor Ethan Westbrook, Sr. and his wife, Ladonna. It's amazing what problems the decision of one person can create for innocent people and how behaviors can be repeated through generations without realizing it. Donovan wanted the chance to be a father, not realizing that his existence on earth had been tainted in more ways than one by the actions and secrets from his father.

Imagine what would have happened if Donovan had been successful in having children with Dominique. They would have been born unknowingly from an act of incest which is rooted in perversion. Donovan's plan for revenge after Dominique wasn't honest with him about the real reason she was barren, gave him the children he wanted, but they came with a price. A price that Donovan couldn't afford one and that ultimately cost him his life, leaving his children without their mother or their father. In spite of what has taken place, there was still a generation left in the earth through Judah, Joshua, Joseph and Justice, and there was still a purpose for them to fulfill. The sin was in the acts committed not the womb that ultimately birthed purpose and destiny into the earth.

To be continued...

www.ingramcontent.com/pod-product-compliance
Lightning Source LLC
Chambersburg PA
CBHW051423150726
48000CB00005B/1935